Also by Crystal Thrasher

The Dark Didn't Catch Me

(A MARGARET K. MCELDERRY BOOK)

BETWEEN DARK AND DAYLIGHT

BETWEEN DARK AND DAYLIGHT

Crystal Thrasher

A MARGARET K. MCELDERRY BOOK

Atheneum 1979 *New York*

Library of Congress Cataloging in Publication Data

Thrasher, Crystal.
Between dark and daylight.
"A Margaret K. McElderry book."
   SUMMARY: In rural Indiana at the end of the
Depression 12-year-old Seely's world is forever changed
when an ominous threat from the Fender twins explodes
into violence.
[1. Family life—Fiction. 2. Country life—
Fiction. 3. Depressions—1929—Fiction] I. Title.
PZ7.T4Be   [Fic]   79-12423
ISBN 0-689-50150-1

Joseph, this one is for you and our kids,
Carol, Joe, and Jan. With my love.

BETWEEN DARK AND DAYLIGHT

chapter one

From where I sat on top of the furniture, it seemed to me that the truck Dad had borrowed to move us and our belongings out of Greene County this Sunday had been stalled or stopped more than it had been moving. We had been on the road ever since daylight and there was still no end to the hills in sight. Whenever the truck was running smoothly and going along at a good clip, Mom got sick at her stomach and we had to stop. Then when Mom said she guessed she felt well enough to go on a-ways, the truck wouldn't start.

Dad had threatened to blow up the truck five times already. The last time, Mom had mumbled under her breath that she doubted if he would know how to, even if he was of a mind to blow it up. She said that Dad didn't know anymore about driving a truck than a heathen knew about heaven. "Which is less than nothing," she muttered.

Once again the motor turned over, caught, and roared to life. Dad gave it more gas, yelled for me to hang on tight, and started fighting the gearshift stick for first gear. Mom held six-year-old Robert close to her chest and braced her feet against the floor boards. The gears clashed into first, and the trucked lunged forward with leaps and bounds like a scared jack rabbit.

I settled myself securely in the nest I had made between the worn rolled-up carpet and heaped-up bedding on the truck and wished for the millionth time today that I didn't have to leave Greene County.

If I was just a little older, I thought, like my seventeen-year-old sister Julie I wouldn't be jiggling and joggling around on a load of furniture like a sack of chicken feed on a farm wagon, leaving everyone and everything I treasured behind me. But I was only a twelve-year-old girl and I didn't have any choice in the matter of where I would live.

Julie had been allowed to stay with friends in Greene County to finish out her last year in high school, and with each turn of the truck wheels, I felt the loss of her company more and more. Now that it was too late to say anything, I could think of a million things that I wanted to tell her. I hadn't even said hurry home nor told her how much I would miss her until she got there.

Dad had said that Julie would be coming to live at the new place where we were going, but I doubted it. I felt deep in my heart that Julie would never find her

4

way to this new home. Just as surely as my brother Jamie, who lay buried beneath the red clay of this dark county and lost to me forever, Julie would lose her way in the hills and hollows and I would never see her again, either. Even her good-bye had sounded more like it was for always than a temporary parting.

I knew it was a fool's wish, but I wished anyway that Julie and Jamie were here with me. They had ridden on the truck with me going to Greene County, and I didn't want to leave without them. Suddenly, my eyes burned, my throat closed tight, and I couldn't breathe. I swallowed hard, but the tightness stayed in my throat and I hurt all the way to the pit of my stomach.

"I wish things were the way they used to be," I sobbed aloud. "I want to have last year back again."

I hadn't cried once while I helped Mom to pack and store our stuff for moving. Even when I waved good-bye to Julie at the old house, my eyes had been dry. But now my face was wet and I didn't try to stop the tears. Let them run free, I thought. There's no one to see me nor to tell me to stop it. It doesn't matter now if I cry.

After a while, I raised my head and let my eyes rest on a spot above the tree tops, and the passing breeze dried my wet face.

The truck was passing through a small village when I again took notice of the country around me. It was no more than a wide place in the road, but there was a big sign at one end of it that read: IF YOU LIVED IN JUBILEE YOU'D BE HOME NOW. Tired as I was of the bumping truck, I didn't wish to live there.

Just beyond the village, Dad stepped down hard on the gas and the truck gave a sudden surge of speed to make a run for the steep hill that loomed ahead of us. About midway up the hill, the steaming radiator finally boiled over, spraying the windshield with water and blurring Dad's view of the road. He stuck his head out the window so he could see until we got to the top of the hill, then he pulled the truck to the side of the road, stopped, and stepped to the ground.

I leaned over the sideboard to ask what we were going to do now. But Mom beat me to it.

"Rob, what do you aim to do now?" She sounded like she was at the end of her patience with him and the truck. "We can't just sit here!"

"There's not one damn thing else to do," Dad replied just as impatiently. "We've got to wait till that damn radiator quits spitting and spewing before we can go any farther."

I crawled over the top of the furniture to the tailgate, jumped to the ground, and went to the front of the truck where Dad was fumbling with the hot radiator cap. He glanced up and saw me and motioned me back, away from it.

When I barely moved, Dad said, "Damn it, Seely, stand back! You'll get scalded if this cap suddenly blows off."

I took a few steps backward and stood at the open window where Mom was sitting with a damp rag held to her forehead. Robert had slid across the seat and was playing with the steering wheel. She took the cloth away, raised her head, and asked how Dad was making out with the radiator cap.

I said he was still trying to get it loose, and turned as Mom did to watch him. Suddenly, Dad jerked his hand back from the radiator cap, swore, and blew on his fingers. "Burned himself," Mom said knowingly. Dad turned from the truck and stomped away, following the twisting track of road farther on downhill.

Dad walked to the first deep bend in the road, the one that would have taken him out of sight, then turned and started slowly back up the hill, stopping every so often to eye the deep gullies and ditches on either side of the road.

"I thought I might find a creek or small stream running down one of those hollows," Dad said, when he stood resting his arms on the open window beside Mom. "But I reckon we'll just have to coast down this hill and hope for a river at the foot of it where we can get water for the radiator."

He turned from the window and nearly stepped on me. He took a deep breath, but all he said was, "Girl, if you're going with us, you'd better get back on that truck."

I scrambled up the slat sideboards like a monkey, and just as I tumbled over the top rail, the truck sputtered to life, and we moved slowly to the center of the pock-marked, rough gravel road.

Dad moved the gearshift stick back and forth from high to low, trying to find neutral and get the truck out of gear so it would coast on its own. There for a

7

while I didn't think he could do it, but then the grinding sound ended as Dad hit neutral, and all was quiet. The truck picked up speed on the downhill grade, and the only sound was that of flying gravel being thrown against the truckbed by the swiftly rolling wheels.

Steam rose from the hot radiator and mingled with the cloud of dust that swirled up behind us. When I looked back, I couldn't see the top of the hill through the thick gray fog.

I felt breathless as though I was flying through space. There was nothing but the sky above me and a wall of trees on every side. I had almost the same free, weightless feeling I used to get when I rode the grapevine swings across the deep ravines from one side of the hill to the other at our old place.

I closed my eyes. In my mind I could see Jamie smiling shyly as he waited patiently on the far hill for his turn to swing. I took a deep breath and held it for the flying swing back to Jamie. Just then the truck hit a chuckhole in the road, and my eyes flew open. I was brought back to earth with a hard jolt. That was last year, I thought. And all of a sudden, the bumpy ride on top of the racing, free-wheeling truck was nothing at all like the breathless swing on a grapevine.

I moved closer to the sideboards so I could face the wind and see where we were going. But just as I reached for a handhold on the top rail, the front wheels hit another big hole in the road and the loaded furniture lurched to one side. Before I could catch myself, a rear wheel hit the same chuckhole, pitching me and everything else that wasn't tied down into the high weeds and thick buckbrush that grew along the side of the road.

The fall must have addled my brains. I could see that the back end of the truck was nearly touching the ground, leaning toward the side ditch as if ready to lie down at any moment, but in my senseless state, it didn't mean a thing to me. Somewhere, far off it seemed, Robert was crying like he was half killed. Dad got out of the truck and hurried around to the other side. Mom just sat there, looking as stunned as I felt. And I lay in the ditch where I had landed and watched them.

Then Dad was beside me, calling my name as if it hurt him to breathe. He put his hands under my arms and stood me on my feet. My knees buckled. "Lean on me," Dad said. Then he called to Mom, "She's all right. Just had the wind knocked out of her."

Mom dropped her head for a moment as if saying grace or giving thanks for an unexpected blessing, then she slid across the seat toward the truck door.

"Is Robert hurt?" My voice came out with a squeak as if it had grown rusty since I'd used it. "I heard him crying. Did he break something?"

Dad laughed without making a sound. The way he did when something pleased him deep down inside. "He's just scared," he said. "Far as I can tell, Seely, there's nothing broken anywhere but that damn rear axle."

He moved a few steps away from me then to help Mom across the shallow side ditch, then reached to take Robert in his arms and set him on his feet next to me.

"Whatever will we do now?" Mom was facing Dad, shaking her head and wringing her hands in agitation.

9

She locked her fingers together in front of her to keep them still, and her voice fell with weariness and disappointment at this further delay.

"You said we'd be there by nightfall," she said. "You promised me faithfully. . . . ."

"You don't have to remind me, Zel. I know what I said."

Dad spoke sharply, breaking her line of thought and putting a stop to her babbling words. Then more quietly, he added, "You can see for yourself, that damn truck ain't going another mile further this day."

Dad swore softly under his breath and kicked the truck tires. Not the flat tire that lay crumpled under the load at the back, but the three good ones. He said by rights he ought to strike a match to the damn thing, burn it to the ground and be done with it.

"Before you do that," Mom said with spirit, "get my trunk off it, and the things Grandmother Curry left to me."

Great-Grandmother Curry had been dead a lot longer than I'd been living, but Mom still took care of her old things just as if she expected Grandmother to walk in at any moment and demand to have them back.

Dad acted like he hadn't heard a word Mom said. He turned from the rear of the truck and began to pick up the pots and pans and the things that had spilled from the split boxes. When he had them all in one place, he straightened up and motioned to a small clearing on the other side of the road.

"We'll make camp over there for the night," he said. "Then come morning, I'll walk to Crowe."

"You'll do no such thing!" Mom said, raising her voice to him. "You'll not leave me stranded in this god-forsaken place with the two young'uns on my hands and no roof over our heads. . . ."

"What would you have me do, Zel?" Dad broke in. "You know I can't afford to lose a day's work." He took a step toward Mom and put out his hand as if to make peace with her. "This Depression seems to be letting up, and times are getting better, but we're not out of the woods yet."

Mom looked at the trees and dense forest that grew to the very edge of the road on both sides of us and said, "Rob, I couldn't have put it better myself."

Dad slapped his hand hard against the door of the useless truck. "You know what I mean, Zel! We need every penny I can make on that job. And besides that," he added, "Hallam ought to know what has happened to his truck."

When Mom didn't say anything to that, Dad went on. "You will be all right here," he said, in the same tone of voice he used to reason with one of us kids. "There's nothing to fear in these woods, and you've plenty on hand to eat."

It wasn't like Mom to give in that easily, but she didn't make any move to resist further. I guess Dad thought it was all settled. That she had come around to his way of thinking.

"It will be for only a day or two," Dad said. "Just until Hallam Henderson can get a man out here to fix that truck. Then we'll be on our way again."

"No, we won't," Mom replied. She drew herself to

her full height, her eyes hot with anger, but her words clear and cold as ice. "You go to Crowe tomorrow and leave me here, and I'm through. You'll go on alone from here."

Mom had always said that Julie got her high temper from Dad, that she was just like him. But at that moment, I could see and hear Julie in every word Mom spoke. She even walks like Julie, I thought, as Mom turned from us and walked away, pushing herself up the hill as if she was bucking a strong wind, and not even bothering to look back.

I hugged myself and shivered in the warm May sunshine. Even during the first hard year in Greene County, when Dad would be gone for weeks on end, Mom had stayed and taken care the best she could. But now, it looked like she meant to shuck Robert and me off on to Dad, and wash her hands of all three of us. I wondered what was to become of Robert and me.

Robert sniffed his tears, choked, and hid his face in my skirt to muffle the sound of his crying. A rush of feeling came over me. Feelings that I was hard put to understand. I had never felt much affection or tenderness for Robert. I thought he was too selfish and too demanding, trying to get his own way about every thing. But now I did. And fast on the heels of this new protective feeling for him came anger at Mom and Dad for making him cry.

Just because they are mad at each other, I thought to myself, doesn't give them the right to scare Robert.

I hugged him closer to me, then squatted on my heels

so our faces were on a level, and watched silently as Mom widened the distance between us and herself.

As we watched, Mom's steps slowed, then came to a stop. Her shoulders slumped forward and her hands came up to cover her face. She stood that way for a moment, then she lowered her hands and lifted her face to heaven.

I had seen her do this exact same thing a million times in my life. Whenever we kids were acting up or Julie had got the best of her in an argument, Mom would raise her eyes to heaven and say, "Lord give me strength." And I guess He did. Afterwards, she could handle anything that came her way. Even Julie.

Mom studied the thick growth of trees off to one side of the road for a long while as if trying to see what lay beyond the shaded woods. Then she turned and walked slowly back down the hill to where we stood waiting beside the truck.

When Mom was within whispering distance, Dad said, "Well, Zel?" As if she hadn't been away.

"Rob, I don't know where I thought I could go."

Her voice was low and I suspected she'd been crying. But when I looked, her eyes were clear and steady, and she was almost smiling as she faced Dad. They just stood there and looked at each other, neither one saying a word. They didn't even seem to be breathing. Just taking the other's measure and liking what they saw. Then Dad reached a hand toward Mom and said, "There's still a lot to be done before dark." And the spell was broken.

"There's wagon tracks up there leading back through

the woods," Mom said then. "They're worn down as if folks are used to traveling the road every day." She pointed to show Dad where the trace of a road left the graveled pike. "We could more than likely find someone there to help us," she added.

Dad's eyes followed her pointing hand, then shifted to where the sun lay just above the tree tops. "We've got about three hours of daylight," he said, as if thinking out loud. Then he turned to Mom. "If it would make you rest any easier, Seely could follow those tracks and see if there's anyone living on that wagon road. While she's gone, we'll unload the stuff from the truck and set up a camp for the night."

He must have noticed the doubtful, defeated look on Mom's face, for when he spoke his voice was low and more gentle than usual. "Zel, there's nothing else we can do," he said. "We're going to be here awhile, so we might as well make the best of it."

chapter two

I started up the road toward the lane that branched off through the trees. Dad said, "Seely, we'll need water." I went back and took a bucket from the pile of things he had stacked beside the truck and started out again. Before I had taken three steps, Robert began to beg to go with me. I stopped and waited until one or the other of them said whether he was to go or stay. Finally, Mom said all right, he could go. "But you keep an eye on him," she told me.

With Robert on one hand and the battered bucket dangling from the other, I followed the wagon ruts into the trees. I could see automobile tire marks in the dust where the weeds were worn away, and I figured the road had to lead somewhere. No one in his right mind would drive a car into the woods, I thought, not unless he was heading for some specific place. If there was a house back here, I wanted to find it quickly and get back to the truck before dark. I took a tighter grip on Robert's hand and walked a little faster down the dirt road.

"I don't care whether we find a house and people or not," I told Robert as we hurried along. "Tomorrow we can walk to the little town of Jubilee that we passed a-ways back and get whatever we need."

"Why do you say that?" Robert asked.

His eyes got big, but he laughed with me when I tugged playfully at his hand and answered, "If we can't find anyone, then we can't borrow from them, can we?"

He shook his head no, and smiled, not really understanding, but pleased that we had shared something to laugh about.

The wagon tracks ran out of the trees into an open field, and we saw a low, rambling old house sprawled at the end of the lane. A faint wisp of smoke rose from the chimney, and a black two-seated automobile was sitting in the yard.

"I forgot it was Sunday," I said. "They've probably got company."

"They've got a mean dog, too," Robert said, as if I couldn't hear the loud barking and growling from up ahead.

He wanted to turn back then, but I said, "A barking dog won't bite. They just bark like that to scare you." I didn't really believe what I told Robert, but it seemed to satisfy him.

The dog's growling got louder and more ferocious as

we opened the gate and started into the yard. A man yelled from the porch and said, "Come on in. He won't bite!" Then he yelled at the dog.

Without getting up, he reached behind his chair for a stick of stove wood and threw it at the dog. He missed. But the dog yelped and leaped away, slinking as far from the house as his chain would allow.

I held on tight to Robert and tried to keep my eyes on everything at once as we crossed the yard. These people that we had found didn't appear to be any friendlier than their mangy dog, and I wanted to keep them all in plain sight.

There were six people on the porch. Two women and a little girl to the left of the steps, and three men to the right side. It looked to me like they had drawn up sides and were just waiting now for someone to start something. I turned toward the left.

An old woman sat hunched in a rocking chair, and a girl, the top of whose tangled, long brown hair barely cleared the chair back, was keeping it moving while the old woman slept. The other woman might have been about Mom's age and would've been pretty if she hadn't looked so tired and worn. She sat in a rickety porch swing, her toes touching the floor every now and then to give the swing a shove, and stared at us.

I stopped at the foot of the steps and smiled at the tired-faced woman. Her face didn't change. I took a deep breath. I'd come this far, I thought, and now that I was here, I would say what I'd come for. If they refused me, I'd leave. It was that simple.

"The truck broke down back there on the road," I

said. "And Dad sent me to get a bucket of water."

No one spoke. The only sounds to break the Sunday quiet were the creakings of the old woman's rocker on the board floor, the screeching chain on the porch swing, and the dog's low growl, which had started again.

"So! The radiator overheated on the hills, heh?"

I jumped as the man's voice boomed out behind me. I turned to face him, my heart pounding as fast as the runaway truck on the downhill grade.

The gruff-voiced man sat in a kitchen chair with its back tilted against the wall, and two half-grown boys, not men yet but maybe sixteen years old, swung their feet from the porch railing. One of the boys favored the man: the same dark hair, blue eyes, and stocky frame. But the other didn't resemble anyone that I could see. He was light and fair with a slight build, and he seemed out of place with these people.

"It did once," I replied, when my heart slowed down to where I could speak. "That's why Dad was coasting down the hill in the first place. But we don't need water for the radiator. Not since the truck hit the big hole in the road and broke the rear axle." I took a deep breath. "Mom needs water to cook our supper."

The man shook his head as if to clear his mind or to test his hearing, one or the other, then let the front legs of his chair come down gradually to touch the floor.

"By God, did you hear that, Linzy?"

He shouted the words, pretty much the same as when he had yelled at the dog, and all sounds ceased. I turned my head to face the other end of the porch.

The woman nodded her head and placed both feet

flat on the floor to stop the to-and-fro movement of the swing. "One of you ought to take her bucket to the well and fill it," she said quietly.

I said, "Thank you," and held out the bucket. But no one made any move to come and take it from me.

"Johnny, do as your ma says." The man motioned to the dark-haired boy in overalls and blue shirt. "Fetch the girl some water."

Johnny gave the man a sullen look, and I thought for a moment that he meant to refuse to do it. But then he slid off the railing and came to take the bucket from my hand. He didn't look at me but glanced over his shoulder and said to the other boy, "Come on, Byron," and started off.

Byron stood up and grinned at me. I smiled back before I thought, then lowered my eyes. But I listened to the whispering sound his corduroys made as he walked by me and felt like I had found one friend here, anyway.

No one spoke after the boys left the porch. Robert and I stood at the foot of the steps and waited, and the others sat on the porch and watched us.

It seemed to me that the boys were taking an awfully long time just to get a pail of water. I should have gone after it myself, I thought. We could have been back at the truck in the time it was taking them to fetch it. I moved from one foot to the other, making marks in the dirt yard with my toes, and wondered out loud what could be keeping the boys.

"I'll go and see."

The man left his chair and went around the house in the direction the boys had gone.

Robert fidgeted and tugged at my hand, fussing to be turned loose. He wasn't used to being still or waiting for anything. Mom had seen to that. But when she wasn't around, I didn't humor him and give in to his every whim. I shushed him now.

"Be quiet," I whispered. "We'll be going in a minute."

Linzy must have noticed his fussing. She pulled the girl from behind the old woman's rocker, and said, "Ednalice, take the little boy and go play on your swing."

Ednalice glanced at the big tree that stood near one end of the porch, then smiled shyly at Robert. An old automobile tire swung from a low branch of the tree, and the mangy-looking dog was chained to the same limb.

"We don't have time to play," I said quickly, taking a firmer grip on Robert.

The girl looked from Robert to her mother, then with a bashful smile for Robert, she moved back to her place behind the chair. The old woman stirred, and Ednalice began once more to rock the chair gently back and forth to lull her.

"Are you folks just passing through?" Linzy asked quietly. "Or did you aim to settle here?"

"We didn't aim to," I replied. "But Dad says from the looks of that truck, we'll probably be here for quite a spell."

The woman didn't say anything, so I volunteered to carry on the conversation. It was better than just waiting.

"We were moving from Greene County to be nearer

to Dad's work when the truck broke down." Then I added needlessly, "Now we're going to camp in the woods beside the road until he can get the truck fixed."

"I figured that much." She smiled and the weariness left her face, making it soft and almost pretty. Even her voice seemed more gentle. "I hope you all didn't have your heart set on getting out of Greene County," she said with a bit of a laugh, "for you ain't out yet."

I told her that I didn't have, but Mom did.

She smiled again and leaned forward in the swing as if she was reaching out to us. "There's an empty house over yonder hill where you folks could take shelter," she said. "It ain't been lived in since Byron Tyson's ma died and Gus took him to stay with his aunt Fanny Phillips in Jubilee. It would need some cleaning, but it'd do till you could be on your way again."

If what she said was true—that we were still in Greene County—I could tell her right now that Mom wouldn't have no part of a house anywhere near here.

Instead, I said, "Yes, ma'am. I'll tell Mom about the house."

Just then the boys rounded the corner of the house, lugging a lard can full of water. The man came along behind them, carrying our bucket.

"This wouldn't last no time," he said, handing me the bucket. "So Johnny and Byron filled the lard can for you."

I stared at the big can of water, then at the man and the two boys, wondering how on earth they expected Robert and me to manage so much water. As if he could read my mind, the man said, "The boys will tote it for you." Then he turned his back on us and climbed the porch steps and went back to his chair.

I glanced at Linzy, wanting to say thanks again and tell her good-bye, but she had leaned back in the swing and closed her eyes. It was as if to her we had already gone, and she had put us completely out of her mind.

chapter three

I led the way across the yard, opened the gate for the two boys and Robert, then waited to latch it behind them. I would let the boys set the pace, I thought. They had the heaviest load. I switched the bucket to my other hand and followed their lead toward the wagon road that led through the woods and back to where Mom and Dad were waiting.

From his place on the porch, the man laughed and called after us. "Hey, Johnny!"

The boys stopped, set the can on the ground, and turned to see what he wanted.

"Should you happen on to Schylar and Sylvester Fender," he shouted, "just drop the lard can and run!" Then he laughed again.

A dark red crept up Johnny's neck and set fire to his face, but he didn't say anything. He and Byron picked up the water can and walked on. The sound of the man's loud mocking laughter followed us all the way down the lane.

"Don't let your pa get to you," Byron said quietly. "You know that Jack's just trying to rile you."

"And he's doing it, too!" Johnny said angrily.

The boys walked along without speaking for a while, then Johnny said, "I've got along fine with the Fender boys ever since we moved here and never had a bit of trouble with them. Then Pa had to get nasty with their ma about the money she owed him for the Watkins Products she bought from him, and I ain't had a moment's peace from them since."

He paused as if thinking about it, then went on. "Pa wouldn't have said a word to Nellie Fender if she'd had a man to stand up for her."

"She don't need a man, "Byron said. "She's got Schylar and Sylvester. They're more to be reckoned with and, I'd say, meaner than most men would be. They'll get even with Jack, one way or another, for the name he called them."

"Pa was mad at Nellie and threw the name bastard in her face to hurt her. He never figured on the boys hearing him or having sense enough to feel insulted by it."

"They know Jack meant to insult their ma," Byron said. "And they'll not let him forget it, either. They'll make him sorry he ever opened his mouth."

"Yeah?" Johnny gave Byron a crooked grin. "They

throw stones at me, start a fight every time they see me, and you say they do it all just to spite my old man." Johnny's laugh was short and bitter. "I've got no quarrel with the Fender boys," he said. "And I can tell you right now, it'll be a cold day in hell when I fight them for him."

"They figure that Jack will fight for you," Byron replied. "And that's the day they're waiting for. They can carry a grudge and wait longer to get revenge than anyone I ever heard tell of. Why, just before you all moved in with Grandma Stoner, when they were just kids, Schylar and Sylvester grabbed our four cats by their tails and bashed their brains out on the barn wall to get even with Dad because he had made them mad about something."

Byron's voice had dropped to a whisper as if he were still seeing the mangled bodies of the four dead cats, or else remembering his dad's anger and horror at what they had done. "Dad told Nellie Fender right then and there that Schylar and Sylvester were dangerous and ought to be put away. But she wouldn't hear of it." He nodded his head solemnly. "Jack Meaders ain't no exception," Byron added. "They got even with Dad, and they'll do the same with your pa."

"That's his problem," Johnny said. "He wouldn't ever lift a finger to help me, and I ain't taking on the Fender boys for him."

Their talk was making me uncomfortable. I didn't want to listen, but I couldn't help hearing every word and wondering what stripe of people I'd come up with.

It wasn't that I was afraid or frightened by the angry dark-haired boy and his quiet, soft-spoken friend, but I didn't relish the thought of being alone in the woods with them, either. And another thing, I thought, if we were apt to meet up with these two Fender boys, I didn't want to be anywhere nearby when that happened.

The sun had dropped behind the treetops and, even in the clearing, it was gray twilight. I knew it would be dusk or nearly dark beneath the trees. I called Robert to me and told him not to run ahead as he had been doing, but to stay close by me. Small as he was, I felt better knowing he was walking beside me, near enough to touch.

As soon as we were in the woods and out of sight from the house, the boys stopped to rest. I took Robert by the hand and moved around to the front of them. Now there would be no one between us and the pike road, in case we needed to run.

"It's a long way to the truck," I said, rubbing the red mark the bucket bale had made on my hand. "You can leave the can of water here and Dad will come and get it."

They looked at me, then at each other and smiled.

"We'll carry the water the rest of the way," Byron said and grinned.

I knew that boys about their age got funny ideas about girls, but until now I hadn't thought much about it. I lowered my head and my eyes lit on my big feet in the scuffed and worn-out school shoes and the limp and faded skirt that hung to below my knees. I knew without looking that my shirt tail had slipped out at the waist, and my straight fair hair—people usually called it white because it was so light—was tangled and standing on end from the wind-blown ride on the truck.

They wouldn't choose a skinny, got-nothing girl whose clothes hang on her like a gunny sack on a scarecrow, I thought. And nearly laughed out loud at the picture I must have made for them.

For just a moment, I wished that I was pretty, wished earnestly that a boy would want to look at me and not feel like laughing at what he saw. Then I felt my face grow warm and pink with shame at my thoughts and silently gave thanks that I was homely and didn't have to worry about what boys thought of me.

I raised my head to see if Johnny and Byron were ready to go on and found that they were looking at me. Sizing me up, I thought, as if they knew what I had been thinking and were just waiting to see what I would do now. They grinned at each other and nodded, then turned to me and smiled.

Their open, friendly smiles caught me unaware. I smiled back at once and felt that, given half a chance, I could get to like these two boys and even be good friends with them. It was as if we had silently found a common ground where we could walk together and communicate comfortably with each other.

"See that path through the trees yonder?" Johnny pointed to where the setting sun touched the ridge of hills to the east of us. "Byron used to live just over that ridge, and the two of us wore this trail going back and forth through the trees from his house to where I live with Grandma Stoner."

He brushed the mane of dark hair out of his eyes and looked every direction except at me. "We ain't used it much lately. Not since Gus moved into town." Johnny scuffed the dried leaves and twigs to one side with his foot, and I could see where the ground had been worn smooth at one time. "It's kind of grown over with weeds now," he said. "But we still know these woods like the back of our hand."

I looked at the trace of path and let my eyes follow its faint line to the ridge of the hill. Then I searched the woods on either side for other signs of their trails through the trees.

"Jamie and I made tracks all over the hills and hollows where we used to live," I said. "The path to the big cave under the rocks was worn as smooth as the clay banks on Lick Crick." Those paths would be washed out by now, I thought, or overgrown with weeds just like Johnny and Byron's tracks. "There's no one left to use our paths." I spoke my thoughts aloud.

"Why not? Did Jamie move away, too?"

Johnny's question reminded me that he and Byron were strangers. They didn't know about Jamie. The kinship I had felt for them a moment ago had been nothing more than the memory of sharing the same kind of adventure in another place.

"Jamie drowned in Lick Crick." I could hardly say the words, even after all this time. "He was my brother," I said.

Without a word, Johnny bent to take up one side of

the lard can and Byron lifted the other side. As we walked along, Byron asked about Jamie, then about Julie, and before I knew it, I was telling him about moving to Greene County from the farm.

"Now just when we were getting used to the hills," I said, "we have to move again."

"Where are you headed this time?" Johnny asked.

"Somewhere in Lawrence County," I told him. "Mom didn't like the last place, and Dad said he wanted to be nearer to his work. Now we're here with a broken-down truck and no place at all to live."

"That's a tough way to go," Johnny said. "When I was a kid, we had to move every time the rent came due. Pa wouldn't work, and Ma couldn't. Not and take care of Ednalice."

He shifted the heavy can in his hand and laughed softly. "Then we came to live with Grandma Stoner, and things began to look up for us. I was just ten years old then." Johnny went on with the laughter still in his voice. "But I remember what Grandma Stoner told Pa the day we got to her house. She said, 'If you don't work, then you don't stay,' and she got him a job selling for the Watkins Company. Pa didn't care much for the notion of working," Johnny added, "but we're still at Grandma Stoner's, and he ain't missed a day's work in five years."

The boys both laughed at the old woman's slyness, and Byron said that maybe Jack was growing to like his work. "Naw, he doesn't like work," Johnny replied. "But this traveling job makes him feel big and important."

29

I was glad to see that Johnny was in a better humor. He seemed to have forgotten about Schylar and Sylvester Fender, and his anger at his dad for taunting him was gone, or at least was hidden.

I wanted to ask questions and find out more about the Fenders and the Meaders family, but I didn't want to rouse Johnny's anger again or have him think I was being nosy. Besides that, I thought, I won't be here long enough for it to matter to me, one way or another.

chapter four

The pike road was in sight when we met Dad coming up the lane to find Robert and me. He held a long, stout stick in his hand, and with every step he struck a hard blow at the weeds like he was killing snakes. Dad looks mean when he's not smiling. And he wasn't smiling. He looked at the two half-grown boys and frowned, then he turned to me.

"I see you've got some water," he said. "I'd say it's about time. You've been gone long enough to dig a well."

"It's not her fault," Johnny said quickly. "We had to clean the lard can before we could fill it for her."

Dad's frown got deeper, and he didn't answer Johnny. He reached for the water bucket I was carrying. "Give me that," he said, "and you run on ahead with Robert and help your mother."

I was happy to hand over the bucket. It was heavy. And when I said to Robert, "I'll race you to the truck," he smiled all over and took off running down the dirt road.

I let Robert stay in front of me on the pike, and he noticed the furniture in the clearing before I did. He stopped suddenly and I bumped into him. He turned to me, his eyes wide and wondering. "Seely, are we going to live here? Even without a house?"

I told him that I didn't know what we were going to do. I was as bewildered as he was at the sight before us. It looked as if the house had just been lifted off the furniture and carried away—roof, walls, and windows—and everything else had been left sitting there.

The beds, table and chairs, and even Mom's rocker and the marble-topped stand table were arranged in the same way as they had been in the old house. Only now, they sat a lot closer together. Dad had made a fireplace among the large boulders, and Mom stood at her workbench, close beside the fire, fixing our supper.

Robert ran to her and put his arms around her. "Mom, are we going to live here beside the road?"

She loosened his hands and turned to set a pan over the fire. "I guess we'll have to," she said, biting her lip. "Your dad says we'll be here till that infernal truck is ready to go again."

I said, "It looks like you've set up housekeeping."

She turned toward me, her face flushed from the heat of the open fire. "What did you expect, Missy? We can't sleep on the ground and eat like savages."

"But what if it rains?"

Mom put her hands on her hips and lifted her face toward' heaven. "Then God help us," she said simply.

I waited a moment, then told her what Linzy Meaders had said about the empty Tyson house. "She said it was right near here. And we'd be out of the weather if it did rain," I couldn't help adding.

Mom replied that she would sit beside the road until the snow flew before she would move into a house around here. "I'm trying to get out of these everlasting hills," she said. "Not farther back into them."

Dad came along then, and I didn't mention anything more about the empty house.

Dad set the water bucket on the workbench, and Johnny and Byron slid the lard can underneath it. "We'll cut through the woods to get home," Johnny told Dad, as he stepped to the edge of the trees bordering our camp. "It's closer that way, and if I don't split some stove kindling before it gets too dark to see the chopping block, we won't get any breakfast." He laughed and turned away through the trees.

Dad said, "Any time I can return the favor . . ." But the boys were halfway up the hill by then.

"I'll remind Jack Meaders to stop here in the morning and pick you up," Byron called back to Dad.

Dad answered and waved his hand to the boys. But it was so dark in the woods that I doubt they even saw his gesture.

Mom faced Dad across the fire. "So you're going through with it," she said, and just looked at him.

I thought to myself that if looks could kill, Dad would be lying flat on his back, dead on the dirt floor of our makeshift kitchen.

Without a word, Dad got real busy filling and lighting the kerosene lanterns and hanging them from tree limbs so we could see to eat our supper. Mom bent over the fire to dish up the potatoes she had cooked with onions and canned corned beef and handed the plates to me to set on the table.

"By this time next week," Dad said, smiling and trying to catch Mom's eye, "it won't matter that you had to spend a few days in the woods."

Mom said she doubted that. She wasn't a bit happy about Dad going off to work and leaving her, with no more thought for her, as she put it, than he gave to that broken-down truck.

Dad replied that times weren't so good that he could throw off on a good job. There were things a man had to do, and work and feed his family happened to be one of those things.

When Dad had first mentioned finding a house nearer to Crowe and moving us there, Mom couldn't have been more pleased. She had said, "Rob, if you'll just get me out of these dark hills and hollows to where I can see daylight, I'll never complain again as long as I live."

But she had forgotten her promise to him in just one day on the road. She had complained about everything. And this time it wasn't Dad's fault, I thought. He had got her halfway between the dark and daylight. And he'd have made it all the way out of the hills if the old truck had stood up to the trip.

When supper was over and the dishes washed and put away, Mom sat down across the table from Dad. "I can't believe we've come to this," she said. "Eating and sleeping beside the road like a band of gypsies."

Dad filled his pipe, taking his time to tamp down the tobacco and light it. I could see his eyes smiling in the glow from the lantern, but if Mom noticed, she gave no sign of it. He motioned toward the beds that had nothing but the trees to shelter them. "Zel, don't be giving yourself airs. The gypsies have things a sight better than we do tonight."

He smiled at her, willing her to see the humor of the situation and silently begging her to join him in his tomfoolery.

"Don't you know," Dad went on, "they have fancy covered wagons to sleep in and painted wooden doors to close against the boogeyman and prowling night animals."

Robert had started to the woods to go to the toilet, but at Dad's words, he began to whimper. Mom said, "Now, see what you've done with all your talk about the boogeyman and wild animals!"

She got up to go to Robert, but Dad put out his hand and stopped her. "Leave the boy be. He's not a baby to be coddled any longer. He's just tired and sleepy like the rest of us."

I went to Robert and walked into the shadows with him and waited while he relieved himself. Dad passed close by us as he walked away into the dark woods, the sound of his steps growing fainter and fainter before they finally faded away entirely.

Mom blew out the lanterns, all but one on the kitchen table to light Dad's way back to camp. "You kids get to bed," she said. "Though it's little or no sleep that we'll get here tonight. I know I won't be able to close my eyes for a minute," she added.

The lantern light didn't stretch from the table to the beds beneath the trees. I got Robert ready for bed, then undressed in the dark and crawled into bed beside him to keep him quiet. He snuffed his tears and slid up close to me as I pulled the covers to our chins to ward off the chill and night dampness of early May. Within minutes, his breathing evened off. He was asleep before his feet got warm against my back.

But I didn't sleep. I lay awake trying to count the stars that looked close enough to touch between the new green leaves above my head. The stars seemed to dance in the sky, frolicking here and there among the tree branches. Whenever I blinked my eyes, they were never in the same spot as before, and newer, brighter stars moved in to take their place among the leaves. I closed my eyes once just for a moment to rest them while I waited for Dad to return. When I opened them again, it was broad daylight.

chapter five

I never knew when Dad came back to camp nor heard him leave the place for work in the morning. But somehow, I knew he had done both. Mom seemed more sure of herself when she called Robert and me to breakfast, as if she had made up her mind to something and was now determined to see it through. I thought that probably she and Dad had talked it over while we slept and come to a like-minded agreement on how we'd live. But I found out differently.

"Seely, you'd better get dressed," Mom said. "Your daddy has rented the empty Tyson house and told those two boys to bring a wagon and move us this morning. They're apt to be here at any minute," she muttered, "and it will be up to me to send them away."

I washed my hands and face in a pan of cold water

and shivered as I pulled on my blouse and skirt over the petticoat I had slept in.

"Then we'll be staying in Byron's old house," I said, as I brushed the tangles from my hair and smoothed it the best I could.

"Seely, you never listen to a word I say." Mom put our breakfast on the table. "When I leave this spot," she said, "it will be to the house your daddy promised me in Lawrence County, not just over the hill to batch on someone else's place."

"But it would be better than this."

"Don't give me any back talk. . . ."

I hushed about the house and sat down at the table with Robert.

"Where's Dad?" Robert asked, as if he had only then noticed that Dad wasn't there. "Doesn't he want any breakfast?"

"Your daddy had a bite to eat earlier," Mom told him gently. "Before he left for work."

After hurrying me to get dressed, as if every minute counted, Mom sat and sipped her coffee as if we had all the time in the world. "I'm surprised that Jack Meaders didn't wake you kids when he stopped to pick up Rob for work," she said. "The man has the natural-born voice of a hog caller." After a moment, she added, "I'm happy to say we won't be seeing much of that man."

Linzy Meaders rode between the two boys on the high seat of the mule-drawn wagon, sitting straight and proud with her cotton print dress tucked under her knees to keep it in place. She jumped from the wagon and waded through the dew-wet weeds to our camp like she was used to doing this every day and didn't even feel the dampness.

She smiled hesitantly and put out her hand to Mom. "You've got a real nice place fixed up here," Linzy said. "Seems a shame to do away with it."

Mom stood with her arms folded across her chest and said she hadn't figured on breaking camp. Rob had seen to it that he was comfortable here, and here she would stay until he came for her.

Linzy said, "It ain't safe for you and the young'uns to be here alone. There's folks hereabouts who would as soon rob you as to look at you."

Mom said we didn't have a thing in the world that anyone would want. And for once I had to agree with her. "But," she added, "they'll be a sorry lot if they try to take it from me."

She lifted the lid of the old barrel-topped trunk that held all her earthly treasures and took out Dad's rabbit-hunting gun. "I've got this for protection," she said, as she laid the shotgun across the foot of her bed. "And what's more, I'm not afraid to use it."

I had never known Mom to touch Dad's shotgun before, let alone fire it. But here she was telling Linzy Meaders that, if need be, she could use it. She didn't appear to be bluffing either. Until I saw the look on Mom's face, I would have bet the gun wasn't loaded, that we didn't even have shells for it. But now I wasn't so sure.

Then Mom smiled at Linzy. "There's no need for you to trouble yourselves about us," she said. "The truck will soon be fixed and, when it is, we'll be going on to Lawrence County."

I knew it would be easier to move the hills than to change Mom's mind, and I guess Linzy Meaders could tell that, too. She turned from Mom and touched my arm feather-light as she passed. "If you need anything," she said, "give me a holler." Then she got into the wagon, clucked to the mule, and drove away up the hill.

chapter six

*J*ohnny and Byron, with
Robert following close behind them, had been fooling
around the old truck while Mom and Linzy were talking. Now they were squatted on their heels staring at
the sagging, lop-sided rear end and the mashed-down
flat tire beneath it.

"What are you boys doing?" I called to them from
halfway down the slope to the road. They glanced up
and waved, then turned back to the truck. I crossed the
road, then stood nearby and watched them as they studied the flat tire.

They grinned at me and got to their feet. "We've
chocked the wheels," Johnny said, moving around to the
side of the truck to show me the huge stones he and
Byron had shoved under the wheels to keep them from

rolling forward. "As soon as we get back from the saw-mill with some props, we'll pry that wheel up and brace it."

"What good will that do?"

"Not a heck of a lot," Johnny replied, and laughed. "But if we can have the rear end jacked up and the tire changed when the men get here, it shouldn't take them long to fix the axle."

We circled the truck, Johnny talking and pointing out all the things that needed to be done to the truck. I nodded my head every now and then as if I knew exactly what he meant. But I didn't understand a word he was telling me.

"Rob said it would be all right for us to mess with the truck," Johnny said, when we had got around again to Byron and Robert. "He said there wasn't any way we could hurt it," he added.

"I guess not." I touched the good rear tire lightly with my toe.

Byron said they had to get started to the sawmill. "Them props won't come to us on their own," he said. They waved a hand at Robert and me and trotted off down the road.

I wished with all my heart that they had asked us to go with them. I knew about sawmills, and we wouldn't have got in the way there. Jamie and I used to watch the men at Ben Collier's sawmill slide the big logs by the whirling blade and listen as the saw bit into the wood with the sound of a million buzzing bees. "If Jamie were here now," I thought, "we could go with the boys. Mom wouldn't even miss us."

When Johnny and Byron had gone out of sight around the bend in the road, I took Robert by the hand and went slowly up the incline to where Mom stood waiting for us. The pie safe with its turquoise-painted face and the white kitchen cabinet looked even more out of place here in the woods, I thought, than Mom's marble-topped stand table and the rocking chair. And I laughed out loud at the sight.

"What's so funny?" Robert asked.

"We are," I said and ruffled his smooth, honey-blond hair. "We're funny."

Mom took the shotgun from the foot of her bed, handling it as if she expected it to go off in her hands, and put it back in the trunk. She closed the trunk lid and, with a deep sigh, slumped down on its humped back. Mom seemed bewildered. Like now that she had taken it onto herself to stay here by the roadside, she didn't have any idea what to do next.

"We'll not be here very long," I said, keeping my voice low and trying to find the words to please her. "If we set our minds to it, we could make this an adventure. Something really special to remember for a long, long time."

Robert moved nearer to Mom, and she put out her hand and drew him onto the trunk lid beside her. "I doubt that we'll soon forget it, either way," she said dryly.

She sat quietly for a moment longer, then got up and went to find the broom. She swept the leaves and broken twigs from the ground as thought it was a pine board floor in our own house. When the leaves were in a neat pile, she threw the broom aside and bent to gather up the litter.

"We'll need firewood to last us through the night," she said, as she tossed the leaves and twigs onto the hot coals of the breakfast fire. "It will be up to you and Robert to see that we have dry wood to burn, some that won't smoke us out of camp."

I didn't say so to Mom, but I thought the smoldering leaves were doing a pretty good job of that right now. I wiped the water from my stinging eyes. I was glad to take Robert and escape into the clean fresh air of the woods.

At first, we stayed close to the road. Then gradually, we ranged farther and farther back into the trees, marking our way with chunks of wood and dead branches. We would pick them up on the way back to camp, I told Robert when he wanted to drag them with us. There was no telling how far we might go or what we might see before we decided to turn back.

Robert talked constantly. Ever since we had left Mom in the kitchen beside the road, he had hardly paused long enough to get his breath between words. Finally, I could stand it no longer. I said, "Slow down, Robert. You're going to run out of wind."

He hushed his talking, but then he began to drag his feet. I started to tell him to step it up, we didn't have all day. Then I realized we had all the time in the world and slowed my steps to fit his.

After a while, we wandered into a deep cove nearly hidden by trees at its entrance and walled up on three sides with great moss-covered stones and boulders. Huge old trees grew up above on the rim also and their branches met over the top, making it dim and shadowy below. Robert and I took off our shoes and walked barefoot over the thick, soft new grass that covered the ground from wall to wall, and then, without speaking one word, we went back to its opening and silently put on our shoes.

There was a feeling of something sacred about such a spot, as if Robert and I had walked on hallowed ground. It didn't look like anyone had ever been there before us, and I wanted to make sure we didn't disturb a thing or make a path to lead others there. Our feet barely touched the ground as we backed away from the trees that hid this secret place.

"That was an adventure for keeping, wasn't it, Seely?"

I nodded my head, answering Robert silently, in hopes that he would be quiet. But he was too full of what he had seen not to talk about it. "That was a sight, pure and simple," he said, the awe and wonder of it still showing in his face and eyes.

Not far from the hidden green cove, we stumbled onto a path and followed it until it came to an end at a narrow dirt road. I stopped and looked in both directions. It was a long way to the bottom of the hill, but just a few steps to the top. Without thinking about it twice, we turned up the dirt road. We weren't even pretending to search for firewood now, we just wanted to see what lay beyond the ridge.

When we topped the rise in the road, we saw that it veered sharply away from the trees and came to a stop in front of a big house, which sat empty and alone in the clearing. Robert and I stared open-mouthed to see such a fine place so far from the main road, and unused.

"I'll bet that's the Tyson house that Linzy Meaders was telling us about," I whispered. Even though there wasn't another soul except Robert to hear me, I felt that this was a whispering kind of place and noise would disturb it.

"Let's get closer and look at it." Robert dropped my hand like a hot potato and started running ahead of me down the lane. I called his name softly, and a few other names under my breath, then hurried to catch up with him.

It was a grand house. It had two wide porches that I could see and each had a solid roof and floor. A faded red pump stood ready and waiting on the porch that faced away from the road toward the barn and out-houses. I wished for a tin cup so we could try the water. Gathering firewood was a thirsty job.

As I went on around the house, I noticed that the doors stood wide open, a silent invitation to anyone who might want to go inside. And I wanted to.

Robert sat on the porch steps and waited for me, his hands clasped around his knees, holding them close together.

"Seely, let's go to the toilet while we're here. I don't like to go in the woods."

"I can't see where it could do any harm," I said. "Since we're here, you go ahead. But hurry," I called, as he started toward the privy.

I went quietly up the steps and through the open door into the house. Dry leaves had blown into the room and been swept into a pile along one wall. A dead bird lay rotting in one corner, and black soot had streaked the wall below the flue hole; other than that, the room was clean.

The floors were wide, bare pine boards, and a border of brown varnish marked the width of the carpet that had once covered them. Wide wainscoting came halfway up the walls, stained with the same brown varnish that trimmed the floor, and a faded blue print wallpaper went the rest of the way to the ceiling. I touched the blue walls, and the paper felt soft to my fingers like old silk.

Robert came in struggling to catch one shoulder strap, which hung just out of reach over his shoulder. I straightened the strap and hooked the fastener to the button on his bib overalls. He smiled his thanks, then stepped quickly away, as if I would hold him or stop him from exploring the empty house.

He couldn't know it, but now that I had seen this much of the place, nothing short of bats, rats, or maybe a bear could keep me away from the rest of the house. We whispered, then held our breath to listen as we tiptoed from one room to the other. There were seven rooms in all, five on the ground floor and two at the top of the long wide stairs. And each of them was fine enough to be a parlor.

I couldn't imagine why anyone would want so many rooms, I told Robert. We couldn't make use of half that many.

"What do you think they used them for?"

"Well . . ." I thought a while. "They probably

cooked in the one nearest the porch with the pump, then ate in another room. They had a parlor just for company, and a gathering room for the family. The other three rooms were where they slept," I added.

Robert was amazed. "Three bedrooms for three people? Seely, I don't believe that. Kids don't have a room all their own."

"Some kids do," I said. "And what's more, all dads and moms don't sleep in the same bed, either."

"They do too," Robert stated positively. "Even if we lived here, Mom and Dad would sleep in the same bed like always, and I'd sleep in a room near you."

I didn't say anything right then. I was wondering what it would be like to have a room with my own bed where I could close the door on the rest of the house whenever I wanted to, and have a place of quiet that I didn't have to share with anyone. I could have all that in this house, I thought.

Robert had moved close to me and stood waiting anxiously for my reply. "Don't fret about not sleeping in my room," I said, pulling him to me. "I wouldn't be able to rest without you near by me. And besides, we're never going to live in a house like this one. Why, our furniture would rattle around in this place like a navy bean in a fruit jar."

Robert laughed and ran happily from one corner to another to show me how he could rattle around the room. Then he came and took my hand. "It is a pretty room, ain't it, Seely?"

He wasn't laughing now, but wide-eyed and serious. "Even without any furniture, I'd like to live here." He waited a while. "I think Mom would like this just fine."

I had forgotten about Mom waiting alone and probably walking the floor worrying about us being gone so long. I shut the back door and led Robert toward the front of the house. "Let's go back and tell her about it," I said.

We closed the front door tight behind us and hurried back toward camp. I was glad that we had left the branches and chunks of wood to mark our way. I didn't have to pay a lot of attention to where we were going but just picked up one piece of wood and another, knowing they would lead us straight back to camp.

chapter seven

I knew in my heart that Mom would say there was no use talking about the house. It was out of all reason. But that didn't stop me from thinking about it and wishing we could live there, even for a little while.

"Seely, leave the wood lay."

Mom's voice brought me up short like a dash of cold water. I had been daydreaming about the Tyson place all the way home and had hardly heard Robert's chatter or felt the weight of the wood, until Mom said, "We don't need a tree trunk in the kitchen."

It was only then that I noticed that we had a kitchen. While Robert and I had been viewing the wooded, moss-covered cove in awesome wonder and admiring the fine big house, Mom had been working to make a walled fort of our camp.

Using the pie safe, cabinet, and workbench to separate the kitchen from the rest of it, Mom had done all she could to make a safe haven where we could live. The beds had been pushed together, the sturdy iron bedsteads forming one wall. The dresser, boxes, and barrels closed in the end. She had left just enough space between the kitchen table and chairs for us to go in and out of the room. A chair could be pulled away from the table to close the opening.

"The boys helped me," she said, when I wondered out loud how she had done it. "When they came back and saw what I was doing, they pitched in and helped as if they had known me all their lives." Mom motioned toward the road. "They're down there now, working on the truck," she added.

Robert dropped his armload of wood beside the fireplace and headed straight for the truck. I was surprised that Mom let him go. Usually she kept Robert close beside her, never allowing him out of her sight for a minute. It was a wonder in the world that she had sent him to gather wood with me.

She had never permitted him to roam the hills and hollows with Jamie and me. When we would ask to take Robert with us, Mom always said he was too little, that she was afraid he would get hurt. But now, here she was, trusting two strange boys to see that nothing drastic happened to him.

Johnny and Byron had set the heavy cast-iron, wood-

51

burning cookstove and the equally heavy heating stove off the truck. A prop that looked like a round fence post was wedged under the rear axle, and the other end of the prop rested on a larger boulder. "To get some leverage," Mom said.

We watched from the camp kitchen while they pried the rear end up. Then the prop slipped and the whole thing came crashing down. The boys bent over their work, doing it all over again. Mom nodded her head in approval and went back to fixing dinner. I took the axe and began to chop the wood we had brought into short pieces to fit the fireplace.

Mom didn't ask what Robert and I had seen or done in the woods, and I didn't tell her. She had worked so hard to make this camp homelike for us, and she seemed satisfied now with the arrangements. I wouldn't upset her by mentioning the big house, I thought. There was no need for her to know about it, and I would just forget that I ever saw it.

But I had forgotten about Robert and his big mouth. We had no more than sat down to our dinner when he started telling Mom about the house we had found on the other side of the hill.

I tried to shush him. But trying to stop Robert from talking, once he got started, was like trying to dam up White River with a handful of straw. The words flowed on and on, while I got more uncomfortable by the minute.

I wished that I had told Mom myself and been done with it. If she had known beforehand, then she wouldn't have listened to Robert. She would have said, "I've heard all I want to hear about that house," and that would've been the end of it. But now, Robert was going on and on, and Mom was taking in every word.

"Seely went inside and made me go with her."

I gave him a dirty look, but he wouldn't even glance my way.

"We looked in every room, but there was nothing inside except a dead bird, and we didn't touch it."

Mom looked at me sternly, and I said, "He's lying! I didn't make him go inside. And besides that, the doors were open."

"That's no excuse to trespass," she said. "I've told you kids time and again, if it doesn't concern you, then leave it be."

Johnny and Byron grinned at me across the table, then looked down at their plates. I don't know why Mom had to ask them to eat with us. It wasn't a bit like her. But she seemed to have taken a fancy to these two boys. As soon as they had stood up and stepped back to inspect the elevated rear end of the truck, Mom had called them to come and eat. And they hadn't refused. Now she was preaching at me in front of them just as if they were part of the family and had every right to hear it.

I knew what was coming next and could recite it word for word. And sure enough, she said it. "Seely, I don't know what I'm going to do with you."

In the silence that followed her words, Byron pushed his plate to one side and turned to face Mom. When his brown eyes met hers, he said, "Mrs. Robinson, that's our house they are talking about. The one Rob rented for you. And it's yours if you want it."

53

Mom said she had no use for a big house and got up from the table, her hands moving quickly as she cleared away the dishes and went to stack them on the work-bench. Then she stopped suddenly and called, "Who's there?"

She waited a moment, then turned back to the table. "There was someone spying on us. Standing behind that tree yonder, near enough to hear every word we spoke."

Johnny and Byron exchanged a look, and Johnny said, "Did you see what they looked like?"

Mom shook her head. "I just caught a glimpse of someone as he was moving away through the trees."

Johnny and Byron pushed their chairs back from the table and said they had to be going. "Ma wanted us to get some things for her in Jubilee," Johnny said. Then, "Do you need anything from the store?"

Mom said she couldn't think of a thing.

"Then we'll see you later," he said, and the two boys went whistling up the road toward town.

I washed the dishes, while Mom carried in the chopped wood and stacked it near the fireplace. "I don't like to think of night coming on and knowing there's someone in the woods watching our every move," she said. But as the afternoon went by, she seemed to forget her uneasiness and moved around camp just as though she was in her own home.

After an early supper, Mom filled the kerosene lanterns and lighted them, placing one on the kitchen table and another on the dresser, lighting up the living area, but leaving our beds in deep shadow beneath the trees.

Later on, when she could find nothing more to do,

Mom piled wood on the fire and, when it was blazing higher than my head, we sat around it and talked and made wishes. Mom wished in a quiet way that we had never left the place in Greene County until we were sure we could get where we were going. "It wasn't much of a house, heaven knows, but it kept off the night dampness," she said.

Robert wished that Dad and Julie were home with us. "I miss them." Then, as if he realized we weren't home, he said, "I'll just wish for morning. I know that one will come true."

I didn't tell my wish. I'd learned a long time ago—last year—that wishing was just a way of passing time, like the old woman's rocking on the porch of the Meaders house.

The fire burned down and clouds covered the moon before Mom stirred from her place and said we should all be in bed. "Must be near ten o'clock," she murmured. But even after we were in bed, she went on telling about the old days when she had been a girl living with her Grandmother Curry. I fell asleep to the sound of Mom's voice and dreamed that I was the little girl who lived at Grandmother Curry's house and that Mom was the grandmother.

Later, I dreamed that a car stopped near where we were, and I could hear men's voices speaking loud and clear. I saw Mom in her long white nightgown standing on the rise between me and the light. She had Dad's shotgun in her hands, aiming it toward the road and daring anyone to approach our stronghold. When I tried to sit up in bed and speak to her, the car went away and the dream changed. In the new dream, I was in the cave above Lick Crick and Jamie was with me. Even in my sleep, my mind was aware enough to think, "Wishes do come true, after all."

chapter eight

*R*ain was hitting me in the face. I turned my head, but I could still feel it. I opened my eyes. Robert's wish had come true. It was morning. But the one thing that we had all wished wouldn't happen was happening. It was raining, and there wasn't a thing in the world we could do but accept it.

Mom stripped the beds and spread the blankets over the tree branches to make a shelter, then started a fire to cook our breakfast. The fire spit and sizzled as the rain hit it, then fizzled out completely. For our breakfast, Mom opened a jar of peaches and we sat on the bed under the blanket tent and ate them.

Robert grinned, with his mouth full of peaches, and

said, "Seely, is this another one of the adventures that you said we'd have here?"

I tilted the dish and drank the peach juice that was left in the bottom of the bowl. "I suppose so. An adventure can be anything that you've never seen or done before. Like the green mossy cove we saw hidden in the hill yesterday, or helping Johnny and Byron work on the truck. Those things were all new and different to you."

"Then this is an adventure," he said.

Mom smiled, humoring us, and said, "I can't see how eating canned peaches in the middle of a wet bed can be much of an adventure, but I'll have to admit it's something we've never done before."

We smiled at Mom, happy to have her going along with our game. And she smiled back. Then Robert followed my lead and tipped his dish to get the last drop of juice. Mom frowned.

"There's no call to forget your manners just because we're living like hoboes," she said. But she wasn't cross. I think she corrected us more out of habit than anything else.

As the rain increased, the leaks in our cover spread from one end to the other. We would move from one wet place only to find that what looked like a dry spot was wetter than the one we had just left. "This is only a spring shower," Mom said. "It won't last long."

But it was still pouring down rain a couple of hours later when Linzy Meaders and the boys drove up in the wagon again. They had a huge tarpaulin pulled over their heads to keep the rain off them.

Linzy jumped from the wagon and came marching up the slope like a woman with a purpose in mind. "You and the young'uns can't stay here in this weather," she said, as she greeted Mom. "And I'll hear no nonsense about it. There's room at Grandma Stoner's and you're welcome to stay till your man comes for you."

She stepped back, as if she expected an argument from Mom. But Mom didn't seem as determined to stay here beside the road this morning. She looked at our soaking wet furniture, her eyes lingering longest on the old humped-back trunk. "I'd hate to leave my things here," was all she said. And she began to make preparations to break camp.

"Then we'll move it all into the Tyson house where it will be out of the rain." Linzy took a firm stand, as if now that the matter was settled, she wouldn't back down for any reason. She seemed like a different person than the one I had talked to on the Meaders' porch. I figured it was because her husband was away. Jack Meaders' odd manner would put a damper on anyone's spirit, I thought.

Mom didn't argue. She even made an effort to help load the wagon, until she slipped on the wet slope to the road and fell in the mud. Johnny helped her to her feet and said if she would just show them what she wanted moved, he and Byron would carry it. She didn't need to lift a finger. Mom stepped aside then. But she was already muddy. We all looked like muddy pack rats as we followed the mule and the heavily loaded wagon down the pike.

Johnny and Byron had tied the tarpaulin over the

wagon to protect our supplies and keep them from getting wetter. But we walked bareheaded through the rain and got drenched to the skin in no time at all. Mud gathered on our shoes and made our feet heavy and clumsy, so we stumbled and dropped things. We would stop every step or so and wipe our shoes on the wet weeds along the road. It took longer, but it was easier than gathering up the stuff we spilled every time we slipped and fell.

Our shoes weren't the only things that collected mud from the road. An accumulation of red clay and gravel stuck to the wagon wheels and slowed the mule and wagon until they were barely moving. Then on the rain-slick rise near the top of the ridge, the mule balked and refused to move another foot.

Byron was driving the wagon. He slapped the worn leather reins on the mule's back and yelled, but the animal paid him no mind. He just braced his legs in the gummy red clay and wouldn't budge a step.

Johnny went to the front of the wagon and took the bridle in both hands, pulling at the mule's head with all his might. But it didn't do a bit of good. He just got mad at the mule and muddy for his trouble.

Mom and Linzy Meaders scraped the wheels clean with strong, sturdy sticks, then braced their shoulders against the back end of the wagon and pushed. The mule seemed to sense that he was getting help with the load and dug in with all four feet, grunting and straining every muscle to move on up the hill.

At first, the wheels barely moved out of the mud ruts, but then the mule found solid footing, and he went to the top of the ridge and over the hump. Once on the other side, the wagon rolled easily down the hill to the house.

Mom barely glanced at the two-storied house that had caught my fancy. She turned to Linzy Meaders and said, "Let's get inside, out of this weather," and led the way to the back door. At the porch steps, she looked at our muddy shoes and said, "You kids clean your shoes." Then she walked through the door, seemingly without giving a thought to the mud that she and Linzy were tracking into the house.

Robert took off his shoes, left them on the porch, and padded into the house barefoot.

Johnny and Byron grinned and wiped the rain from their faces with their wet shirt sleeves. "Let's get the stuff off the wagon," Johnny said and turned from the shelter of the porch to where the mule waited, head down and still breathing hard from the long pull.

The rain dwindled to a sprinkle as Johnny, Byron, and I carried everything from the wagon and piled it on the porch. Mom and Linzy moved it into the house. We had the wagon nearly empty when the rain stopped all together, and a weak, watered-down sun showed itself through the clouds.

Linzy Meaders said now that the sun was out, it would be warm in no time at all. But I figured if I waited for that little bit of sunlight to take the chill out of my bones, I'd be cold for the rest of my life. I fished through one of the boxes for an old flannel shirt of Dad's and put it on over my wet blouse.

Mom said it was pure foolishness. The dampness would

seep into the shirt and I wouldn't be any warmer than I was before. But I folded the shirt across my chest, hugged myself to cover the fullness, and told her, "I feel better, already." She just shook her head as if to say, "Have it your own way," and left the room.

Johnny was driving the mule and wagon when they started back for the rest of our things. I watched them for a moment, then closed the kitchen door quietly behind me. This time I wasn't waiting to be asked, I thought, and ran to catch up with the wagon.

Byron reached to help me over the wheel, then scooted to the middle of the seat to make room for me. I sat on the very edge of the board seat fiddling with the buttons on Dad's old shirt, watching the steam rise from the hide of the sway-backed mule. I wondered why I had ever wanted to ride along with these two boys in the first place. After Byron had helped me onto the wagon, he had turned his face toward the road, talking to Johnny and completely ignoring me. As far as they were concerned, I thought, I might just as well have stayed at the Tyson house with Mom and Linzy Meaders.

I could tell just as soon as the truck came in sight that someone had been there while we were away. The back end seemed to squat on the ground, leaning more than ever toward the side ditch, and broken glass covered the road in front of the truck. Someone had smashed the headlights.

Johnny's face was grim as he slapped the mule across the rump and urged the animal up the hill at a faster pace.

"I knew it was those blasted Fender twins that your

ma saw watching us yesterday," he said. "And now they've been here doing their dirty work already."

Byron said, "There's no use to hurry. The damage has been done." Then with a sidelong look at Johnny, he added, "If it was the Fenders, Schylar and Sylvester will be long gone by now."

"No, they won't," Johnny replied. "They wouldn't go to all that trouble to get a rise out of me, then not stick around to watch the fun." He pulled the mule to the side of the road and jumped to the ground. "They're probably hiding up there amongst the trees right now, laughing their fool heads off at us."

Byron crowded by my knees and over the wagon wheel to the rain-filled side ditch. "Then we'll fool them," he said, laughing softly as he offered his hand to help me from the high seat. "We'll load this stuff and head back to the house just as though we don't see a thing wrong with the truck."

Johnny didn't think much of the idea, but he went along with Byron's suggestion. The boys laughed and joked as they carried the awkward coiled bedsprings to the wagon and loaded the heavy cast-iron stoves, turning down my offer to help, while they put on a sideshow for an invisible audience.

While they were playing the fool, and slipping and sliding on the muddy slope to the road, I buried our empty tin cans and potato peelings, then scattered wet leaves over the scarred earth where we had been living. An hour later when we drove the mule and wagon down the hill, away from our camp, only the useless, broken-down truck remained to show we had ever been there.

63

When we were midway up the hill on the mud lane, Byron and I got off the wagon and left Johnny to guide the mule while we pushed. And if the Fender boys were watching us, as Johnny and Byron seemed to think, they didn't show themselves.

Mom and Linzy were unpacking dishes and putting them away when we got to the house. They had already set up two beds for Robert and me in one room, the room I figured the Tysons had used for a parlor, and the frame was together, waiting for the bed springs, in another room off the living room.

I said, "Why are you making beds and unpacking dishes? I thought we were going to stay at the Meaders' house till Dad got home."

"I can't see any sense in our piling in on Linzy," Mom replied. "Now that the furniture and all our things are here in this house, we might as well wait here for your daddy."

After they had shoved the heating stove into a far corner of the front room and set the cooking stove under the flue hole and fitted the pipes in place, Johnny and Byron told Mom about the damage to the truck.

"I sure hope Rob ain't held accountable," Johnny said. "Cause that truck ain't worth a plugged nickel now."

"Even though it was a no-good thing to begin with," Mom replied, "the truck was loaned in good faith, and Rob will be honor-bound to make it right with Hallam Henderson."

She asked Linzy and the boys to stay and eat a bite

before they left, but Linzy said they had to get on toward home.

"Grandma Stoner is real good to keep an eye on Ednalice," she said. "But I can't trust her to start a fire and get supper ready."

They were halfway to the wagon when Mom called, "I'm much obliged for all your help," and hurried after them. "I want to pay you something for the use of your mule and wagon."

Johnny stopped and turned to wait for her. "That's all been taken care of," he said. "Rob paid us real good to do all this before he left for Crowe."

chapter nine

*T*he sky clouded over again in the late afternoon. Before dark, Mom sent Robert and me to carry in wood and water to last the night.

"The house is cold and damp," she said, "and we'll need to keep a fire in the cook stove to take some of the chill from our beds."

Mom seemed more uneasy about staying in the Tyson house that night than she had been about sleeping under the trees beside the pike road. She moved restlessly from room to room, bolting the doors, checking the window catches, covering the bare glass with sheets and blankets and whatever else she could lay hands on.

When I yelled at Robert for meddling in my things, Mom hushed me with a harsh whisper. "Keep your voice down, Seely. There's no need to tell the whole countryside that we're here alone," she said.

"There's not a soul for miles around to hear me."

But I kept my voice low. Maybe I was wrong.

Mom didn't light a lamp until she had shoved the straight backed kitchen chairs under the doorknobs as an extra precaution. Then she turned the wick down until the light was so dim we could barely see across the room. There were no stories that night about the olden days, nor any special wishes for impossible things. As soon as supper was over and the dishes put away, Mom said it was our bedtime. And if we knew what was good for us, she added, we'd go to bed.

"I've made a pallet on the floor beside my bed for you and Robert. You'll sleep there tonight." Then, as if answering my question before I could ask it, she said, "If I need you, I don't want to search a strange house in the middle of the night to find you."

Mom brought the lamp into her bedroom and we went to our pallet, but it was too early to go to sleep. Robert whispered in my ear, then giggled when I covered my head. He turned first one way and then the other, taking all the covers with him.

"Shut up and lay still!" I whispered, but it came out louder than I meant it to.

Mom had gotten into bed by this time, too. "Both of you hush!" she said.

I yanked on the blanket, getting my half and Robert, back on my side of the pallet. After that, everything was quiet.

Suddenly, Mom sat up in bed and whispered, "What was that noise?"

I said I hadn't heard a sound.

"Well, I did," she stated flatly. She threw back the covers and got out of bed. "It sounded to me like an automobile just stopped in our yard."

My eyes had grown used to the dim lamp light and I could see every move Mom made. She went directly to the old trunk, took out Dad's shotgun, then checked to make sure it was loaded. I sat up and started to get to my feet. "Stay down, Seely," Mom whispered. "And be quiet."

She picked up the lamp, carried it to the kitchen, and blew out the light, leaving the house in pitch blackness. I couldn't see her, but I followed the sound of her bare feet as she tiptoed toward the kitchen door.

I heard the scrape of wood on the floor as Mom slid the chair from under the door knob, then the soft click of the bolt unlocking the door.

"Don't open the door!" I leaped to my feet and ran stumbling through the dark toward her. I threw myself against the door, bracing it with my body as I fumbled for the bolt to lock it again.

"Get out of my way," Mom said. "I'm just going to scare them."

"You're scaring me!"

I slid the bolt, locking the door, just as strong, heavy hands hit the door from the other side and the knob turned.

Mom shoved the chair back beneath the knob, and we

68

leaned against it, Mom hugging the shotgun, and I too frightened to move.

"Damn it, Zel. Open this damn door!"

"Rob." Mom breathed the name, and the chair and the shotgun landed on the floor as she unbolted the door and swung it wide open.

"Oh, Rob!" She sounded like she was laughing and crying at the same time. "I wasn't expecting you."

Dad struck a match and held it up, looking around the room. Then he stepped to the table and lit the lamp. He grinned at Mom when he saw the overturned chair and the shotgun on the floor. "What were you expecting?" he asked. "An Indian attack?"

Then he laughed.

I think it was the laugh that did it. Mom flared up at once, lashing out at Dad to relieve the tension of the past few minutes.

"For all you know about this godforsaken place, it could've been!"

Then she seemed to remember the sound that had scared her so in the first place. "Where did you get an automobile?" Without waiting for Dad to answer, she said, "Borrowed it, I suppose. Though I can't feature a man loaning his car in times like these."

Dad said, "Zel, when you're through speaking your piece, I'll explain about the car."

Robert had come running to the kitchen as soon as he had heard Dad's voice and was hanging on to him now, pestering him with questions. Dad said, "Be quiet, son. Give me time to get my coat off."

He looked around the room for a hook or a nail where he could hang his coat and cap. When he didn't find one, he threw them on the table and sat down, settling back in his chair.

"Now, I'll tell you how I come to have that car," he said to Mom, almost defiantly, it seemed to me. "I bought it. Laid out cold cash from the sale of the house in Greene County for it."

You could've heard a feather hit the floor in the silence that followed Dad's words. Mom stood with her mouth open, as if she'd had the breath knocked out of her and she was incapable of saying a word. Robert and I just waited quietly to see what would be the outcome of it all.

Mom rallied almost at once, and when she got her second wind, she started reciting all the things we needed, and a car, she said, was the last thing. "Rob, you must've taken leave of your senses to waste good money that way," she ended.

Dad replied quietly that the car was no waste. He felt that he couldn't go on forever depending on a ride with just whoever happened along to get him to work. Even after we moved to the house in Lawrence County, he would need an automobile for the hour's drive to and from work each day. He looked at the angry lines in Mom's face, and said, "There's no use carrying on about it, Zel. Troy Michael had this Buick touring car for sale, and I needed transportation. We made a deal, and it's all settled."

"How do you figure to settle with Hallam Henderson

for his truck?" Mom asked then. "It's going to take every penny we can lay our hands on to pay . . ."

"Hallam's got insurance," Dad interrupted her. "He said I wasn't to worry about the truck. He'd turn it in to his insurance company and they'd handle everything."

I'd never heard of a company that would pay a man for wrecking his truck, but it seemed to satisfy Mom. She dropped the subject of the car and asked Dad when Hallam expected to have the truck fixed so that we could move on.

"He'll get a mechanic out here as soon as the insurance company settles up with him," Dad replied. "It might be a month or six weeks from now," he added. "Those things take time."

"A month!" Mom had gone to the stove to warm some leftovers to give Dad for his supper, but now she slid the pan to the back of the stove so it wouldn't burn and turned all her attention to him. "*Six weeks?* Rob, we can't afford to pay rent on two houses—not when one of them is standing empty. That would be like throwing money down a rat hole," she added.

Mom stopped to get her breath, and Dad spoke up, trying to calm her. "We'll manage somehow, Zel," he said gently. "I promised you that house in Lawrence County, and you shall have it. But it will have to wait a while," he added. "Hallam's truck is our only hope of getting moved there."

"And while we wait," Mom said sharply, "you'll be paying out money for a house we can't use."

She turned back to the stove and pulled the pan of

71

leftovers onto the heat again. Suddenly, her shoulders slumped forward and her head drooped. All the anger and fighting spirit seemed to have gone, leaving Mom as flat and empty as a punctured balloon.

"Give up that place in Lawrence County," she said softly, not looking at Dad while she spoke. "I couldn't rest at night knowing I was a party to such a waste of money."

Mom raised her head to face Dad and seemed to see Robert and me for the first time since Dad had walked into the house.

"Seely"—Mom pointed toward the front room of the house—"take up that pallet. Then you kids go to your own beds."

Dad slid Robert off his lap, got to his feet, and went to pick up the overturned chair and his shotgun.

I turned to do Mom's bidding, but she called me back. "Take a lamp with you. You'll not be able to find your way in the dark."

I lit a lamp and carried it to the room I was sharing with Robert and set it on the dresser between the two beds. I left the door open so it would light my way across the front room to Mom's bedroom, then went back to gather up the quilts and blankets from the floor beside Mom's bed.

Robert came to our room while I was putting the extra bedding away and without one whimper, he climbed into his own bed and pulled the covers up to his chin. "I'm going to sleep fast tonight," he told me. "I want to get up before Dad goes to work so I can see the car."

"Me too," I answered, and blew out the light.

72

I was almost asleep when Robert whispered, "Seely, do you think we'll get to ride in the car sometime?"

"I don't know," I said. "But it's more than likely." I heard his contented sigh as he turned on his side to sleep.

chapter ten

*T*he rattling of the stove grate as someone shook down the ashes and laid kindling to start the breakfast fire woke me the next morning. It wasn't daylight yet, but the black of night had faded to a pearl gray, and I knew dawn wasn't far off. I lay in bed for a moment, getting my bearings in the strange room. Then I got up, found the door, and followed the slim line of light to the kitchen.

As I stepped into the room, Dad struck a match to the kindling, closed the firebox door, then turned to face me.

"Seely, what are you doing up at this hour?"

"I wanted to see the car you bought before you left for work."

Mom came in from outdoors while I was speaking and

stopped at the washstand. "Go on to bed," she said, dipping her hands into the washbasin and splashing cold water on her face. "You can't see much of that car in the dark and, besides, you need the sleep."

Dad said, "Oh, leave her be, Zel. It does a young'un good to see the sun rise now and then."

"But I just wanted to see the car," I told him.

"It's not much to see," Dad said, his smile touching me like a blessing. "But it does have good tires, and the motor sings like a bird." He turned toward Mom as he added, "I figure there's a lot of good miles in the old bus, yet."

But Mom was measuring coffee into the pot and gave no indication that she had even heard him. She'd made it clear last night how she felt about that automobile, I thought to myself, and she wants him to know she hasn't changed her mind.

Breakfast was a quiet one, broken only by Mom asking if Dad wanted more coffee and what would he like in his dinner bucket. I waited until he had finished eating and set his dinner pail on the table. Then I went in to wake Robert.

"Come on," I said, giving him a good shake. "Dad's leaving for work."

For just a moment, his blue eyes were blank and blurred with sleep. Then they cleared as he remembered why he wanted to get up early. He leaped out of bed, pulling up his pajama pants so he wouldn't trip over the legs, and ran ahead of me to the kitchen.

Dad had spoken the truth when he said the car wasn't much to look at. It wasn't. The pale blue leather seats were ripped and torn at the seams and the stuffing bulged out like a split sausage. The cloth top was so ragged and full of holes that it wouldn't have kept off the tiniest sprinkle of rain. But the bright sky-blue paint was shiny and pretty. Not one scratch or dent marred its smooth finish. And when I tried the doors, all four of them opened and closed with just a touch of my hand.

"Don't swing on the car doors," Dad said. And I stepped back, away from the car.

"We can put that top down and cover the seats with a blanket, and you'll never see the holes," Dad told Mom, as he stepped back to admire the car. "The new paint job it had not so long ago looks fine."

"But I'll know they're there!" Mom replied shortly.

Later that week, Linzy Meaders came over to see if Mom would walk to Jubilee with her. "I thought you might need something from the store," Linzy said, dropping into a chair at the kitchen table. "And no one likes to walk alone into a strange town."

Mom said that Linzy shouldn't have gone out of her way. "But now that you're here," she went on, "if you don't mind waiting while I measure the windows in that front room, I'd be much obliged to go with you."

Linzy got up and followed Mom into the other room. "It looks real homey," she said. "But you do need blinds at the windows."

"I hadn't thought of getting shades for in here," Mom said. "My mind ran more toward bright curtains for this room."

She and Linzy studied the windows for a moment, then Mom took a tapemeasure from her apron pocket and stretched it the width of the window. "I didn't figure on staying here long enough for it to matter about the curtains," Mom went on, "but when Rob said it might be weeks or even months before that borrowed truck would be ready to move us, I decided to give up the house in Lawrence County for now and concentrate on making this one more comfortable."

She gave Linzy a sidelong glance with just a bit of a smile, as if she were taking Linzy into her confidence and passing on private information. "Rob saw fit to buy an automobile to drive to work. So I said to myself, as long as I'm here I might just get a few nice things for the house."

There was a new note in Mom's voice when she spoke of the car. She complained about it, but it was more of a token complaint than anything else. She seemed to think it was expected of her, so she did it. And she knew too that the Watkins Company furnished Jack Meaders with an automobile to deliver their products, while Dad owned the car he drove to work. She didn't want to seem better than Linzy.

In the midst of talking to Linzy, she turned and said that Robert and I should get our shoes on if we were going with her. "Can't have folks thinking you don't own a pair," Mom said, then went on talking.

We were both ready to go by the time they had finished measuring the windows in the front room.

Just over the hill from our house, we left the road

and took the path that Johnny and Byron had made through the woods to the Meaders' house. Then before we got there, we turned onto another path that bypassed their house and brought us to the pike road midway up a long hill above Jubilee. It was the same hill where the radiator had boiled over on the truck. But if Mom noticed, she made no mention of it.

At the edge of town, Linzy threw up a hand in greeting and called, "How are you?" to the woman doing a washing on the back porch of a weather-beaten old house.

The woman straightened up from the tub and washboard and wiped her soapy hands on her hips. Then she pushed the mane of red hair out of her eyes and smiled when she saw who was calling to her. She didn't speak, but lifted a hand and waved.

"Nellie Fender," Linzy said as we went on by. She lowered her voice and added, "Nellie stutters. It takes her a while to get her words out."

"Is Nellie Fender Schylar and Sylvester's mother?"

Linzy gave me an odd questioning look, and I added hastily, "Johnny told me about them. He said that Schylar and Sylvester slashed the tires and busted the headlights on the old truck Dad drove down here."

"That's more than likely the truth," Linzy answered. "They're a couple of hellions, and I wouldn't put it past them. But Johnny had no business accusing them unless he was sure of it. There's enough hard feelings between the Fenders and us the way it is," she added.

I didn't say anything to that. I was thinking that if

the motor had died when the radiator got hot, or the truck had broken down on this hill, I would have been sent to the Fender house for help. The thought made me shiver. From all I had heard of Schylar and Sylvester, the less I had to do with the Fenders the better I'd like it.

"Nellie Fender is a good woman," Linzy was saying, "even if she doesn't go to church. Until that day when Jack had a fuss with her about money she owed for some of his products and got the two boys down on us, I used to stop every Sunday night to ask her to go to prayer meeting with me. She never went," Linzy added, "but I enjoyed talking to her on my way there."

We had left Nellie Fender well behind us, but she was still on Linzy's mind. "Grandma Stoner says that other than working for Gus Tyson's wife before she died, Nellie always kept to herself. Everyone around here was surprised when she had them twin boys. She was just a young'un, then."

"If she was too young to be a mother," I said, "then why did she have them?"

Mom gave me a stern look, but Linzy didn't seem to notice. "Nellie had no choice in the matter," she replied.

We had reached the general store while Linzy was speaking, and I had no time to ponder on her words. But they did strike me as an odd thing to say about anyone. I couldn't believe that even Nellie Fender didn't have the right to choose whether or not she would be a mother.

Inside the store, Linzy made Mom known to Abner Griffin, the storekeeper, and told him what we needed.

"They've just rented the old Tyson place," Linzy said, "and Mrs. Robinson is here to buy new curtains for the parlor."

"I don't handle no ready-made curtains," Abner Griffin told Mom. "But there's some yard goods yonder that might serve your purpose."

He pointed to the far wall of the store, then reached for Linzy's list with the same hand and began to fill her grocery order.

Mom didn't even glance at the well-stocked food shelves in the store, but made a beeline for the dry goods counter and the stack of bright colored material. She murmured under her breath that she wanted curtains that wouldn't clash with her dark burgundy carpet and, after taking down several bolts of material, she chose a bolt of pale pink cotton with a deep rose-colored flowered pattern.

I'd never seen a flower that even slightly resembled the one on the roll of cloth, but it was pretty. I told Mom that I thought it would go real well with the carpet. Then I kept my fingers crossed, hoping she would buy it. If she took the whole thing, I thought, there would be enough left over to cover the window in my bedroom as well.

Mom bought the entire bolt of pink and rose-colored cotton and a few packets of flower seeds, paying for it all with a twenty-dollar bill. I had never seen that much money before and I was surprised that Mom had it. But I was even more amazed when the storekeeper gave Mom quite a few bills and a handful of silver for her change. It looked like all the money in the world to me.

As we were leaving the store, Mom hesitated beside the flats of vegetable plants that covered one end of the porch, paying special attention to a box of hardy-looking tomato plants.

"If I had a garden spot plowed and worked down," Mom said, with a wistful look at the plants, "I'd take a dozen or two of these home with me."

"Why, Zel, that's no drawback," Linzy said. "Johnny and Byron can bring the mule over to your place tomorrow and break the ground in no time at all."

Mom handed the bolt of cloth to me, then stooped to pick up a flat of tomato plants.

Mom went back into the store, and as the door closed behind her, Linzy said, "I'm real pleased that your ma will be staying on at the Tyson house for a spell."

I smiled and hugged the heavy curtain material to my chest. "So am I," I said.

We kept to the gravel pike road on our way back. Robert complained that he was tired with every breath and every step he took. We climbed the hill slowly and stopped to rest after we had passed the Fender house. There wasn't a soul to be seen on the place, but a week's washing was flapping and drying on the clothesline.

"Everybody else around here does their washing on a Monday," Linzy said, and laughed. "But Nellie Fender does hers whenever the notion strikes her."

Mom gazed thoughtfully at the house for some time. "She can't have had it easy," she said quietly. "Going against the grain of the neighbors, and raising those two boys alone."

"She ain't been entirely alone," Linzy said. "Aunt

Fanny Phillips, Gus Tyson's sister, has stood by her. Fanny sees to it that Nellie has help if she needs it."

We rested awhile longer, then went on, with Robert walking even more slowly now than he had before we stopped to rest.

Before we got to the wagon road that led to the Meaders' place, Linzy had Mom's word on it that she would walk to prayer meeting with her on Sunday evening. Everyone from miles around came to hear Reverend Paully, Linzy said. He wasn't the usual run-of-the-mill preacher. He had the spirit.

As we started on down the road, Mom said, "Seely, I didn't see a church house in that town, did you?"

I said no, but that I hadn't been looking for one, either.

She glanced at me quickly, her eyes searching my face to see if I was being sassy. I guess she was satisfied that I was just stating a fact, for she said, "It's of no matter. We'll be going with Linzy Meaders and she knows where to find it."

Mom made peanut butter sandwiches to hold us over until supper, then spent the rest of the day sewing the new curtains for the front room. Every time the thimble slipped or she pricked her finger with the needle she would stop, take a deep breath, and say, "I wish to heaven that I had one of those treadle sewing machines." But even without a pedal machine, Mom had the curtains gathered, hemmed, and hanging at the windows before dark.

She folded the long strip of left-over curtain material,

then stood quietly smoothing the creases with her hand. "One of these days," she said, "I'm going to make pillow cushions for my rocking chair to match the curtains."

She seemed so happy that I didn't have the heart to mention the hopes I had held for the pink remnant.

I could use the old eggshell lace curtains, I decided, as Mom lifted the top of the trunk that held her treasures and placed the soft pink cotton inside. If I puckered the panels just right, the holes wouldn't show. From a distance, they'd look almost good as new. And that's what I did.

chapter eleven

Dad didn't come home that night even though he did have a car to drive back and forth to work. Mom said he probably had to work overtime, and it wouldn't pay him to make the trip. But she kept supper warm for him. "Just in case," she said.

I don't know if it was the walk to town with Linzy Meaders or that Mom just felt more at home in the house, but she seemed more at ease now. She still bolted the doors as soon as it got dark, but she didn't barricade them. And there was no fuss or nonsense about where Robert and I would sleep when it came to our bedtime. Mom had closed off three of the rooms in the house. But after Robert and I were sent to bed, I heard her checking the windows in the empty rooms on the second floor, then closing the stair door firmly behind her when she came back down.

When we had moved into the house, and our beds were set up, I had unrolled my notebook and put it under the strawtick on my bed for safekeeping. Now that it looked as though we had settled in here to stay, I thought I should make note of the fact.

As soon as the bedroom door was closed and Robert had fallen asleep, I got out the notebook and started writing. Thoughts chased through my mind like mice scurrying to find a hole to get out. But I couldn't put them all on paper. There wasn't enough room. The notebook was nearly full now, and I had to save space in case something important happened.

I read over what I had written, then added, "Dad bought a car. Our first one. And Mom says we don't need it. But she bought tomato plants and flower seeds, and we don't have a garden. We're not out of Greene County, but it looks like we'll be staying here anyway."

I had almost finished writing when Mom said, "Seely, are you reading in bed?"

I called back that no I wasn't. But she must not have heard me. She said, "You'll ruin your eyes. Blow out that light and go to sleep."

I blew out the light and got into bed, but it was a long time before I went to sleep. I thought of the days and weeks and months of summer ahead of me and wondered what I would do for someone to talk to. I couldn't talk to Robert. He was too young. And besides that, he liked the sound of his own voice too well to listen to anyone else.

I thought of Johnny Meaders and Byron Tyson. They seemed to be my best bet, my only hope so far for someone to buddy with. And that was a mighty slim hope. Johnny seemed too busy keeping out of his dad's way and out of sight of the Fender boys to pay any attention to me. And Byron wasn't much better. After that first day when he had asked about Julie and Jamie, and we had talked about where I used to live, it seemed to me like he had said more to that stupid mule than he had to me.

Just as I was dozing off to sleep the thought came to me that all wasn't lost. Not yet. Maybe there would be girls my age at the prayer meeting to which Mom said we were going on Sunday night. With luck, I would find a friend among them.

Johnny and Byron not only plowed a garden spot for Mom the next day, but they stayed and helped us break up the clods of dirt and work the earth down for planting. When we were finished, Mom brought out some money and tried to pay them for their work. But they refused it.

Mom said, "Take the money. You've earned every penny."

They just shook their heads and moved away, keeping their hands stuck deep in their front pockets.

Mom put the money in her apron pocket. "At least

have something to eat before you go," she said, and went up the steps to the kitchen.

Johnny and Byron sat on the porch with us and ate peanut butter and jelly sandwiches that Mom made and washed them down with orange Kool-Aid. Byron said if Johnny had his guitar, we could have music while we ate. Mom went inside at once and brought the battery radio to the porch and let the boys turn the dial till they found some music they liked.

Usually, to save batteries, the radio was only turned on for the news and weather reports. But I guess Mom figured the plowing was well worth a new set of batteries for the radio.

As the boys were leaving, Mom said, "Johnny, bring your guitar over some Saturday night and play us a tune or two. Rob would enjoy hearing some good guitar picking."

Johnny said he would do just that some Saturday night, and he and Byron went whistling off up the road.

It was then that I noticed the two men watching our house from the woods that bordered the clearing. They were standing back in the shadow of the trees, and I probably wouldn't have seen them, but the setting sun touched their hair like a brush fire when they stepped out to follow Johnny and Byron, and the flash of color caught my eye.

They didn't hurry after the boys, as they would have done had they wanted to catch up with them, but hung back in the shade, keeping their distance so as not to be seen.

I called Mom's attention to the two strangers, pointing out to her that they seemed to be following Johnny and Byron on the sly.

"Seely, you let your imagination run away with you," she said. "Anyone with half an eye could see they are just a couple of boys passing by. Boys not much older than Johnny and Byron," she added.

"But watch them! They're sneaking by, not passing!"

I turned toward the woods where I had last seen them for another look at the strangers. But they had disappeared from sight among the trees.

Maybe, like Mom said, she didn't hold much stock in my fancies, but that night she bolted the doors early, and the light was still burning when I went to sleep.

chapter twelve

Dad came home early Saturday afternoon. He had no more than cleared the door, when he told Mom to get her apron off, they were going to town.

Mom untied her apron strings and slipped the loop of the bib over her head. "To Jubilee? Then I can pick up a few cabbage and sweet pepper plants from Ab Griffin's store."

Dad shook his head. "You can get whatever you need in Oolitic."

Mom questioned him silently with her eyes, and he explained sheepishly. "A state trooper stopped me on my way home. I've got to get a driver's license. And he'll be waiting in Oolitic to test me for it."

Mom had gone dead white at the words "state

trooper." "You mean to tell me he arrested you? That you had to pay a fine?"

"It was nothing like that, Zel. The man just said that if I aimed to drive a car—and I told him that was my intention—then I'd have to get a permit and be licensed."

"But you drove Hallam Henderson's truck without a license," Mom said, turning toward the front room. "Did you tell him that?"

"The thought never crossed my mind," Dad said, as he followed Mom to the other room.

I finished washing Robert's face and hands, and we started to our room for a clean shirt for him. Just as we passed through the front room, Dad noticed the new curtains at the windows.

"Good-diddly-damn, woman!" he shouted, glaring at Mom, then at the windows. "Are you trying to put us in the poor house?"

I thought Mom would be crushed. That all her pleasure in the bright new curtains would be dashed away by Dad's disapproval. But for once, Mom didn't back away from his anger. She looked him straight in the eyes, and said, "If we go to the county poor farm, Rob, we'll ride up there in style. That is," she added, "if you can pass that driving test today."

I pushed Robert ahead of me into our room and closed the door. His eyes got wide with fright as he listened to the sound of Mom and Dad's loud voices that seemed to bounce off the walls.

"Don't be scared, honey," I told him, as I lifted him to the side of my bed and sat down beside him. "It's nothing to be frightened about. They're just yelling to let off steam. It doesn't mean that they are mad at us."

I knew quite well how Robert felt right then. It seemed such a short time ago that the sound of Dad's voice raised in anger could send me running in terror to the attic room that I had shared with Julie, or to the hillside cave above Lick Crick. Just any quiet place would do where I couldn't hear him yell and swear. I had thought then that I hated him.

But sometime between then and now, I had grown to like Dad. I'd come to realize that his swearing and shouting were just as much a part of him as the color of his eyes and his quiet laughter. We had nothing to fear from Dad's yelling, I told Robert. And neither did Mom.

The shouting had stopped now, and the house was quiet. But I still sat beside Robert and waited for one of them to call us. Robert took my hand and I separated his fingers, playing this little piggy went to market on each one, starting with his thumb and ending at his little finger.

He looked up from his hand and smiled a watery grin as Mom opened our door and said calmly, "You young'uns come on now. Your daddy is ready to leave for town."

Robert slid off the bed, still holding my hand, and we followed Mom out to the car.

Usually, the holey seats were covered with an old blanket, but today Dad had covered the seats with Mom's patchwork quilts and folded the top back on the car. He had spoken the truth, I thought to myself, as I looked at the shiny blue Buick. No one could really tell now that the seats were split and losing their stuffing or know for sure that the top was full of holes and apt to fly apart at the first high wind. The car didn't look the least bit tacky.

Dad sat behind the wheel, impatiently racing the motor, while he waited for us to get seated. He leaned across the front seat and opened the car door for Mom, then smiled and settled back behind the wheel as she slammed the door firmly behind her.

Mom sat stiff and straight with her pocketbook on her lap and her hands folded together over the top of it. Robert and I sat close beside each other in the exact middle of the back seat. Dad engaged the gears and the car moved slowly up the dirt lane and over the hill to the graveled road.

Even on the pike road, Dad drove slowly, carefully avoiding the ruts and chuckholes and keeping the automobile well over to the right hand side of the road. At the foot of a long crooked hill, he stopped at the edge of a wooden bridge that stretched across a wide river that flowed through the deep cuts in the hill and on down the valley.

"There's White River," he said. "It's wider and deeper here than any place else I know of."

I sat forward on the seat and leaned over Dad's shoulder, fascinated by the rolling, muddy water and wondering how it could ever get out of such high banks to flood the country the way it did after every hard spring rain. There must be two White Rivers, I thought. And it was the other one that did all the flood damage.

"Is this the same one we saw in Greene County?"

Dad laughed. "Seely, we're still in Greene County, and as far as I know, there's just one White River. It meanders all over southern Indiana," he said. "Don't know where it has its beginning. but eventually White River runs into the great Ohio River."

We sat silently at the bridge, each of us enjoying the sight of the mighty river, the green hills, and the pasture land that it cut through to get to the Ohio River that Dad said was many miles away. Finally, Dad put the car in gear, and I sat back in my seat. We crossed the river at a snail's pace, with the loose wooden planks of the bridge floor clattering behind us.

Soon after we had crossed the bridge, or so it seemed to me, we came to the city limits of Oolitic. Dad parked the car in front of a big stone building, took his billfold from his hip pocket and counted out some bills, which he gave to Mom.

He pointed to the grocery store further down the street on the other side and said. "I'll pick you and the young'uns up at the Rainbow Store when I'm finished here." He watched closely as Mom tucked the money deep inside her pocketbook for safekeeping. "Take your time doing the trading," he added. "I may be here for a while."

Mom got out of the car and walked away as if she was the Queen Mary of England, or a very close relative, and Robert and I tagged along behind her.

As we went down our side of the street, we passed a tavern with a sign that lit up and said BEER. The place smelled of mold and mildew. Next to it sat a three-story house where they sold old books and odds and ends of everything. Old furniture and junk were piled high on the front porch, and a table loaded with dishes that didn't match sat in the yard, close to the sidewalk.

I stopped to look at the pretty dishes, but Mom kept her eyes straight ahead and didn't break her stride until she came to the corner. Robert was plodding along about halfway between the two of us, but Mom looked back, called my name, and waited until we caught up to cross the street to the other side.

Across the street, the Rainbow Store, a hatchery, and a feed mill sat as close together as three in a bed and seemed to look down their noses at the two buildings facing them from the other side of the street.

I said that I thought the second-hand store and tavern had a lot more character than a hatchery or feed store, be it for animals or for people. But Mom told me to stay away from those two places, and, furthermore, she didn't want to hear any such talk again. She held the door open and motioned for me to go ahead of her into the grocery, lest I shame her by even glancing across the street.

Mom took a shopping basket and hung it over her arm. But she didn't put anything in it. We just wandered up and down the aisles looking at all the stuff on the shelves and watching what the other women were putting in their baskets.

I heard someone call my name and turned just as Johnny and Byron stopped beside us.

"We saw Rob across the street and he said you were

here doing your trading," Johnny said, eyeing Mom's empty basket.

Mom was searching the aisle behind him and just half listening. "Did Linzy come to town with you?"

"Ma and Pa are both in town," Johnny replied. Then with a sly grin, he added, "But they're not together. Ma went to the bank, and Pa's having a beer at the tavern."

Mom's lips thinned at the word *tavern,* but she seemed real interested in the bank. "You mean to tell me this little town has a bank?"

"There's a main street one block over," Byron said, motioning with his hand. "It has a bank, post office, five and ten, and a drug store." He paused for breath, looked at me, then blurted out, "We came to see if the kids could have a soda with us. It's just around the corner," he added.

Mom must have had something else on her mind and only halfway heard Byron. She didn't hesitate for a moment to think it over. "I suppose so," she replied, and turned away to get on with her shopping.

I couldn't believe that Mom was letting Robert and me out of her sight in a strange town. Especially not with two boys that she had known for less than a week. But I didn't wait to question her decision. As we started out the door, she called, "Mind you, meet me back here within the hour."

As soon as the door closed behind us, Johnny said, "That's some automobile your dad got himself. But ain't it a bit sporty for an old man like Rob?"

"Dad said he bought it because it had good tires and the motor ran like new," I told him. "I don't think Dad knows that he's too old for it."

Another automobile parked along the street caught Johnny's eyes, and he and Byron stopped to look it over. While they were admiring the car and running their hands along the shiny chrome trim, I looked at the pretty dresses and fine furniture shown in the store windows.

I could hear the boys talking and whistling through their teeth as they wondered out loud how it would feel to sit behind the wheel and drive a car like that. I was wondering too. But not about automobiles. I thought, just once, I would like to know how it would feel to wear a dress like the one on the store dummy and live in a house where the furniture was new and all the pieces matched.

"We'll never know," Johnny answered for us all. "Only the real rich people can afford something like that."

As we walked on up the street, I thought, For a little while there, we were rich. We could look at these things and touch them. And it was a pleasant feeling to know that even if we couldn't own them, we could look at them and wish.

"In here," Johnny said, taking Robert's hand as he opened the door to the drug store. He led the way to a round table near the window and lifted Robert to a chair that faced the street. "Now you can watch the people," Johnny told him. "That's why everyone comes to town on Saturday, just to watch the people pass by."

Almost the first people to saunter by the window were

two tall, redheaded, freckle-faced boys. I'd never seen two people who looked so much alike, and at first glance I thought I was seeing double and said so.

"That's the Fender twins," Byron said. Then he added, "Aunt Fanny told me she was bringing Nellie to town to pay her spring taxes today, but she didn't mention that Schylar and Sylvester would be with them."

I stared at the Fender twins, wanting to see these two boys that I had heard so much about, and none of it good. They glanced our way at the same time, and I saw their blank amber-green eyes staring back, but not seeing me. As if they looked always inward, not caring to see the outside world around them.

But then their odd-colored eyes lit on Johnny Meaders, and the blankness went away. The look they gave him was so hate-filled and spiteful that I felt as though something evil had passed through the window and touched us all. I shivered as I watched them turn and walk away.

There must have been something familiar about the way they walked or else it was their bright, bushy hair. "I've seen them before," I said, speaking my thoughts out loud. Then I remembered where I had seen Schylar and Sylvester Fender. "They were the ones I saw watching our house the day you were there to plow our garden," I said. "I only saw them for a moment as they stepped from the trees to follow you when you left for home."

"That sounds like something those clods would do," Byron said.

Our sodas came while we were talking. Robert had

to sit on his knees in the chair so he could reach the tall straw.

"They were always thick-headed, even when we were kids," Byron went on. "But lately, they've turned sneaky-mean with their denseness."

Johnny laughed shortly. "Nellie used to bring Schylar and Sylvester to the Tysons' with her when she came to do the housework. I was always there with Byron. They were a couple of years older than we were, but they'd do the dumbest things. Then whenever we would object or say we were going to tell on them, they would threaten us with all kinds of trouble and torture."

He laughed again, then added, "We never did call their bluff and tell Nellie. Stupid as they were, they might have gone through with some of it."

Robert took a deep drag on his soda straw and it made a loud slurping sound that could be heard all over the store. Johnny and Byron laughed.

Johnny said, "Do you know what that means?"

Robert shook his head, the surprised, puzzled look still on his face.

"It means that the glass is empty." Johnny laughed again and lifted Robert from the chair to the floor.

I thanked the boys for our sodas. Byron said, "Glad you liked it." Then he added with a laugh, "It was your dad's money that paid for them."

No more was said about the Fenders. And I was glad. They frightened me. Even though Johnny said, "If they'll leave me alone, I'll sure not bother them," I felt that sooner or later he would have no choice in the matter. The look Schylar and Sylvester had given

Johnny promised nothing but trouble for him in the future.

We'd been gone more than the hour that Mom had allowed us, so we didn't dilly-dally on our way back to the Rainbow Store. And it was a good thing for us that we didn't.

Dad was sitting in the car waiting, and Mom was pacing up and down in front of the store when we got there. Without a word, Mom pointed to the car, then went over and got in. Robert and I said good-bye to Johnny and Byron and climbed into the back seat. They waved, and I heard them say, "See you," as Dad gunned the motor and drove away.

"I got the permit to drive," Dad said, first thing off the bat. "The license takes a while," he explained. "But I passed all their tests and I'll get it later."

Mom smiled, just as pleased and proud as Dad about the driving permit. But she couldn't leave it lay. "Slow down, Rob, and watch the road," she said. "Being allowed to drive a car is a privilege not to be taken lightly."

Then Mom went on to say that she had gone to the bank with Linzy and to the post office to buy stamps and penny post cards. "I had it in mind to write Julie and tell her where we had settled." She didn't mention why she had wanted to go to a bank.

Robert chattered on and on about the things he had seen in town, but I closed my mind to his words. I was silently putting together the letter that I would write to Julie. She would be happy to hear that I had found two friends so soon. But she might think it a bit odd that my friends were boys three or four years older than I. Julie will understand, I thought. She'll know that when there are no girls around, you have to make friends out of the boys.

I smiled to myself as I wrote the next line of Julie's letter. She would think it funny also when I told her that I hadn't been looking for friends when I found Johnny and Byron. All I had wanted then was a bucket of water.

chapter thirteen

 D ad said that as long as Mom seemed bound and determined to go to prayer meeting that Sunday evening, he would drive her there in the car and pick her up after the service. The automobile was sitting there, he said, and he couldn't see any sense in not using it.

But Mom said, "Not the first time, Rob. I wouldn't feel right about it."

"Don't be a damn fool about this, Zel," Dad said, getting red in the face and raising his voice to her. "For once in your life, let your head save your feet a step or two."

Mom just looked at him for a moment, then she said quietly that since she was here to stay, whether she liked it or not, she would get acquainted with the neighbors in her own way. "And it's a cinch," she said, "I'd never get to know them by waving as I passed them by in that automobile."

We left Robert at home, and Mom and I walked to Jubilee.

At first, Mom set a fast pace for us. But as we neared the Meaders' house, her steps lagged, and we just poked along up to the gate.

Jack Meaders yelled, "Come on in," over the noise of the barking dog and offered Mom a chair on the porch.

Linzy said she was ready to go. She just wanted to go inside and get her pocketbook. "Nope, you don't want to forget your money," Jack said to Linzy's back. "The Reverend Mister Paully wouldn't let you through the door without it." Then he laughed as if he had made a great joke.

I didn't like the way he laughed. It wasn't a happy laugh, yet it wasn't exactly cruel, either. Just an odd sound in between the two that set my teeth on edge, and I couldn't quite name it.

We had left the house far behind us before I found the courage to ask Linzy about Johnny. "I thought he would be going to prayer meeting with us," I said.

"Johnny went home with Byron yesterday, right after we got back from Oolitic," Linzy told me. Then she turned to Mom, and said, "Seems like lately, he just can't stand being in the same house with his pa. He'll be coming home with us after the service," Linzy went on in a happier tone. "And no doubt, Byron will be with him. Whenever you find one of those boys, you can be sure the other one ain't far behind." She kind of laughed. "They've been that close since the first time they ever laid eyes on one another," she added.

Mom replied that Linzy was right fortunate in that respect. "You gain by the help they can give you around the house, not to mention the pleasure that having a couple of boys on the place can bring you." She paused for a moment, and I knew from the catch in her voice that she was thinking of Jamie as she went on. "It would be good to be given another boy, even if he wasn't born yours," she said. "Much better that way than to start with two and then lose one along the way."

Linzy's eyes were soft as they touched Mom's face, then quickly glanced away. "Zel, I dare say you're right about that," she said quietly. "Don't know what I'd do without them."

Nothing more was said about the boys, and a few minutes later we came to Nellie Fender's house.

"It don't look like there's a soul at home," Linzy said. But she went through the gate anyhow and up the path to the door. She knocked a couple of times and waited. When no one answered, Linzy came back to the road.

"That's funny," she said, shaking her head. "Nellie is always at home." She looked back at the house and shook her head again, thoroughly puzzled about Nellie Fender.

But when we moved on down the road, and I glanced back at the house, I was pretty sure that I saw the movement of a curtain hastily pulled into place to cover the window.

It wasn't quite dark yet when we reached the schoolhouse where Linzy said the prayer meeting was being held. Jubilee didn't have a church house, she told Mom. So while school was out for the summer, the Reverend Paully used the schoolhouse to hold his prayer meetings.

Several women stood just outside the entryway, and I had the feeling that not one of them had taken their eyes off us from the time we had come into view until we stood there before them.

Linzy Meaders said, "Sisters, I've brought Zel Robinson and her girl Seely to hear the Reverend Mister Paully preach tonight."

Mom smiled and spoke, and the next thing I knew she was being hugged and kissed and God-blessed by every woman there.

Mom had stiffened her back and tried to pull away after the first embrace, but other arms claimed her and she was passed around from one woman to another until the bell rang calling them in to worship.

There was a dazed look on Mom's face as the last woman dropped her arms and stepped back from her. "I'm Fanny Phillips," she said, smiling at Mom. "Byron Tyson's aunt."

Mom took the hand she offered, then Fanny Phillips and Linzy Meaders led Mom into the meeting house and urged her down the aisle to the very first row of seats.

I stopped near the door and looked around the room. There were a few kids at the front with the old people, but most of the young ones had found seats as near as they could get to the back door. I saw Johnny and Byron sitting on a bench in the very last row. They waved and moved over to make a place for me to sit with them.

I noticed one thing right away: there were no girls my age here. And if there were any in the neighborhood, I sure hadn't seen one of them.

The prayer meeting began with singing and a short prayer, just the same as the Sunday night service at the Flat Hollow Methodist Church in McVille. But where the singing left off and the preaching began, it was all different. It wasn't anything like the prayer meetings that Mom used to take Julie, Jamie, and me to every week.

It seemed to me that the first time the Reverend Mister Paully paused to catch his breath, the sermon got out of hand. The congregation got to their feet and shouted, "Amen, brother," and "Yes, Lord," while the preacher waved his arms and tried his best to outshout them.

I looked at Johnny and Byron, intending to ask what was going on here, but they were both watching me with sly, mischievous smiles, waiting to see how I would take all this. I kept my mouth shut and thought to myself, I'll just wait and see what happens.

At first, it looked as though the preacher was trying to bring the meeting to order. But when the crowd clapped their hands, shouted, and swayed back and forth in time to his words, I decided that he was just egging them on.

I shivered in the dim lantern light and was glad I had taken a seat as far as possible from the Reverend Mister Paully.

I thought he was a frightening figure. He appeared to be about ten feet tall, with piercing dark eyes and long black hair that barely cleared the collar of the black swallow-tailed coat that hung on his thin frame like a cornfield scarecrow's. Even in the dim light, his eyes seemed to catch and hold everyone spellbound as he spoke of the hellfire and brimstone that awaited each of us. And he made it sound as if it hadn't long to wait. Probably tonight.

But I guess I was the only one the Reverend Mister Paully scared with his looks and words. When he raised his bony hands and motioned for the people to come forward, to come to him, they rose to their feet at once and stumbled down the aisle, chanting and babbling words that I couldn't understand.

Johnny whispered, "They've gone into their trance. They're speaking the unknown tongue. Anything is liable to happen now."

I watched open-mouthed and scarcely daring to breathe, as a stout middle-aged woman got to her feet, gave a high piercing wail, then pitched forward to the floor and lay there still as death. No one seemed to notice that her skirt was hiked up to her waist and some bare pink flesh was showing.

That is, no one except Johnny and Byron. They nudged me and giggled. "You've not seen the half of it yet," Byron said. "Wait till they really get going."

A child rose and placed a baby blanket over the woman's nakedness, and at the same time a commotion broke out at the front of the room.

Somehow, I knew that Mom was at the bottom of the disturbance, even before I saw her struggling to get out of her seat and into the aisle. As she shoved and elbowed her way through the swaying bodies, someone reached for her, trying to get her to sit down. But Mom struck the hand away and moved ahead like a big fish swimming upstream against the current, and making a beeline for the open door.

Her face was dark with shame or anger, I could see from where I sat, but I couldn't tell which. As her flashing brown eyes darted from side to side, searching for the sight of me, I felt like scrunching down between Johnny and Byron so she couldn't see me. But when she found me, I stood up. She pointed to the door, and I moved to meet her.

Mom waited for me in the aisle. She grabbed my arm, said, "Come on!" then pushed me ahead of her through the door.

The night air felt cool to my face, but it did nothing toward cooling Mom's temper. Her feet barely touched the ground as she swung away from the makeshift church house and down the pike road toward home.

If a record time had been set for walking from Jubilee to the Tyson house, I'll bet Mom broke it that night. She spoke bitterly of the cavorting and carryings-on under the guise of worshiping the Lord and whipped herself every step of the way for ever going there in the first place. "Someone should've told me they were Holy Rollers," she said.

I didn't try to answer Mom. Most of the time, it was all I could do to keep up with her.

When we entered the house, Dad looked up from the book he was reading, glanced at the clock, and said, "You're home early."

"And not a minute too soon to suit me," Mom answered. She was still breathing hard from our fast walk home. "I want no part of their Holy Roller revivals. Women wallowing on the floor, making fools of themselves, and showing everything they've got to God and everybody." She had to stop to get her breath again.

Dad closed his book, keeping his finger between the pages to mark his place. "Zel, they didn't say it was the Methodist meeting house," he said quietly.

"And no one bothered to tell me that it was the meeting place for a pack of heathens, either!"

Mom stormed out of the room muttering something about taking off her good church clothes.

The lamplight struck Dad's face as he turned toward me, and I thought I saw the trace of a smile on his lips. "Seely, what did you think of the Jubilee prayer meeting?"

Tell the truth and shame the devil, I thought. Then I told Dad how the people and the meeting had struck me.

"I thought the women seemed really nice until the preacher got them all stirred up," I told him. "Then they acted like that passel of hogs the time they ate the grape leavings from Mom's grape jelly."

Dad laughed quietly, his eyes crinkling as the smile spread over his face. "You'd better get to bed, now," he said, motioning toward the closed door to my room. "All your mother needs tonight is to hear you having nightmares about that Holy Roller preacher, and she'll never let us hear the last of it."

The minute I had closed my door behind me, I got out my notebook, thankful that I had saved some space for a time such as this one. I thought the whole evening was something worth keeping, and I wrote it all down, ending with a postscript: "I wonder what happened after we left the revival."

chapter fourteen

The next morning Mom was short-tempered and just generally out of sorts. I gave her a wide berth as I went about the house gathering up the dirty clothes and separating the colored pieces from the white ones. I figured by the time the clothes were sorted and ready to wash, she would be in a better frame of mind. Instead, she grumbled as she went to the backyard to build a fire under the tub of wash water.

"Washday comes every Monday," she sighed, "whether we feel like it or not."

And, I thought, whether we like them or not, we have beans for supper every washday.

Early in the morning, Mom would put two cups of navy beans in the big iron kettle with a chunk of bacon for seasoning, then fill the pot with water and set it on a back burner. While the unbleached muslin sheets and underwear boiled in a copper kettle on the front of the stove, the beans would cook slowly on the back lid.

Every washday, Julie used to tease Mom at the supper table and say that she could tell even without looking that Mom had done a washing. She said the beans always tasted like the bluing and the strong brown soap that Mom had chipped from the cake into the clothes boiler. Mom would deny it and swear up and down that it was just Julie's imagination. The next washday she would cook beans again.

Now, while Mom was looking over the beans this morning, tossing bits of stone and bad beans into the woodbox and keeping the good ones to put in the kettle, I strung the clothes line from two tall posts in the back yard.

It was a new rope line and Mom said I would never be able to draw it taut enough to hold a wash. But with Robert swinging on one end of the rope to take up the slack, I managed to tie it really tight. I had just given the line a final tug to test it, when a car came over the hill and coasted to a stop in front of our house.

Robert ran toward the house, but I held my ground until the woman got out of her car and came across the yard. We met at the steps to the back porch.

"Come on in," I said. "Mom's in the kitchen."

She smiled at me, and I knew then that I had seen her at the prayer meeting. But there were so many women there last night that I couldn't put a name to the face.

"I'll just sit here in the sun for a minute," she said and sat down on the top step. "You can tell your ma that Fanny Phillips is here to see her."

I let the screen door slam shut behind me as I went to the kitchen, and a handful of beans rattled against the side of the iron kettle as Mom lost her patience with me.

"Seely, how many times do I have to tell you . . ."

"Mom, Fanny Phillips is sitting on the porch," I said, putting a stop to her scolding. "She wants to see you."

I wondered how Mom would greet Byron's aunt. She seemed to have one face and manner that she used for us at home and an entirely different one that she showed to friends and neighbors. I was anxious to see which one she turned toward Fanny Phillips now.

Mom set the beans to one side, brushed her apron, and went outside. I followed her, making sure to close the screen door softly behind me.

Fanny Phillips got to her feet and just stood there smiling. "I wanted to get over to see you before now," she greeted Mom. "But when Byron told me that you'd be at the revival last night with Linzy Meaders, I made up my mind to wait and see you there."

"What did you want to see me about?" Mom asked. "Was it anything to do with this house?"

"Oh, my, no," Fanny replied. "I just wanted to ask you to go to church with me next Sunday."

Mom's face turned red, and I thought she would choke on her answer. But when she spoke, the words were civil enough.

"I thank you kindly," she said, not smiling. "But what

I saw and heard of the Holy Rollers last night will do me for a while."

Fanny Phillips laughed heartily. A sound that started deep inside somewhere and just rolled out.

"You all think I meant another revival meeting?"

"Where else could you mean?" Mom came back shortly.

I could tell that Mom was holding her temper by a short rein and I was afraid it might break loose at any time. I moved to the edge of the porch near Fanny Phillips.

"We didn't know there was another church," I said. "No one told us about it."

Fanny smiled at me, but her shoulders still shook with held-in laughter. "Law, child, I'm not a Holy Roller. Though," she hastened to add, "I don't fault those who hold with that belief." She turned to face Mom and went on in a more serious tone. "I'm a hard-shelled Baptist, myself. Born and reared one. Our pastor holds forth at the Shiloh Baptist Church every Sunday morning and Sunday night, but he doesn't draw the crowd that the Holy Roller preacher pulls in. Why," she added, "for the young folks, that's more fun than the moving picture shows."

I glanced at Mom, hoping now that she knew about the Shiloh church house, she would be more cordial toward Byron's aunt. But Mom didn't seem to be listening. Something had drawn her attention to the field across the road. I turned to follow her gaze, then just stared at the two tall gangling boys and the red-headed woman who were headed straight for our back yard.

Fanny Phillips murmured, "I wonder what brings Nellie Fender and her boys here at this hour." Then, with genuine pleasure, she called, "Come right on over, Nellie, and say howdy to your new neighbors."

Nellie came slowly toward us, walking like one whose cross is almost more than she can carry but doesn't dare to lay it down for fear its weight might be more than she could ever lift again.

The nearer she got to the house, the farther the boys lagged behind her. She turned once and spoke to them. I couldn't hear what she said, but when she jerked her arm forward in a swinging arc, there was no mistaking her meaning. Schylar and Sylvester Fender dropped their heads lower and didn't answer Nellie. But they stepped livelier after that and got to the porch steps at about the same time as their mother.

Nellie Fender nodded to Fanny, but it was to Mom that she spoke. Haltingly, and with many pauses to get out the words, Nellie told Mom why she had come over to our side of the hill, as she put it, and why she had brought her boys.

"My boys, Schylar and Sylvester here, they want to make it right, what they done to your truck," she said, stuttering and stumbling over her words to make Mom understand. The boys got as red as a turkey gobbler's snout and shuffled their feet while they waited impatiently for Nellie to get on with it.

"I told them that they would chop your wood, cut the grass, and do anything else that needs doing, or that you want done, until the debt's paid off." Nellie sighed with relief to have it said and waited for Mom to comment on it.

In the first place, Mom told Nellie, the truck didn't belong to us. Dad had borrowed it. And there wasn't any question about who would pay for the damage. The owner had insurance. Mom spoke the word insurance as if it was a blanket to cover all problems and cure all ills.

Nellie Fender didn't seem to understand, but Fanny Phillips nodded her head as if she knew all about insurance. She did seem surprised though to hear that an old truck like Hallam Henderson's was insured.

While the three women were talking and trying to decide what to do about the boys, Schylar and Sylvester waited. They sneaked a look at Mom and Fanny, and when they thought no one was watching them, they took to their heels, fleeing from our yard toward the safety of the woods.

"Now, you two, wait just a minute," Fanny Phillips called sharply. "Come right back here!"

They stopped, then turned and dragged their feet back to where the women stood waiting for them.

"It's best that we don't let them off free and easy," Fanny said quietly to Mom. "They'd just use the time to get into more meanness."

She spoke of Schylar and Sylvester right in front of them as if they were deaf or in the next county. And for all the attention they paid to what Fanny was saying, they might as well have been both.

Between the three of them, Fanny, Mom, and Nellie Fender connived to find enough things that needed doing to keep the twins occupied at our house for quite a spell. Then Nellie got in the car with Fanny Phillips and rode away, leaving us to cope with Schylar and Sylvester and put up with having them underfoot for the rest of the day.

At first, whenever Mom asked them to do anything they just stared at her, their amber-green eyes blank as a wall. Then somehow, Mom figured out which one was which and started calling them by name. After that, they paid attention when she spoke to them.

Even at the end of the day, I still couldn't tell them apart. But I kept my eyes on them and stayed out of their way.

They carried the wash boiler to the yard, emptied the water, chopped wood and corded it, then raked up the wood chips for kindling. Mom said they worked good. But she had to tell them every whip-stitch to keep busy or they would stand and whisper to each other, then snicker as if they knew an amusing secret that no one else knew about.

When we had our noon meal, they took their plates to the far end of the porch. Robert wanted to sit and eat with them, but they chased him away.

Robert was disappointed. He came back to the table and sat next to me. "I wouldn't have bothered them," he said. "I just wanted to look at them. I've never seen an exact pair of boys before like Schylar and Sylvester," he added.

Mom must have used their eating time to think up some other things to keep the boys busy. They had no more than licked their plates, when Mom went outside and said, "I think these windows could stand a good cleaning." She ran her fingers across the glass pane and frowned at the dust on her hand.

"Schylar," she said, "bring me the ladder from the barn. We'll do these windows today."

By this time, the boys were grinning at Mom whenever she spoke to them. They didn't say much, but they grinned a lot.

Mom went inside to get the vinegar water that she used to wash the windows. Schylar and Sylvester loped off toward the barn and came back carrying a long wooden ladder. They leaned the ladder against the side of the house, then one of them took the vinegar water from Mom's hands and started up the rungs. While one of them washed and wiped the windows, the other stood on the ground and held the ladder to steady it.

That night as they were leaving, Mom called each of them by name, and said, "I'll look to see you here in the morning." Then, when they were out of the sound of her voice, she sighed deeply. "I wish your daddy was here. He'd know what to do with them. Lord knows, I don't."

All things considered, I thought Mom was handling them pretty fair. And I told her so. But she just shook her head and said, "Oh, I don't know about that."

chapter fifteen

*W*e didn't see Johnny
or Byron all that week. I suppose they had heard from
Linzy and Aunt Fanny that the Fender boys were working off their meanness at our house, so they didn't come
near us.

Mom wouldn't go to the Meaders' house because she
said she didn't fancy leaving Robert and me alone with
Schylar and Sylvester. But she wouldn't allow us to go
either. I reckon she figured since she had to put up with
their smirking, we might as well, too. I was glad when
Friday night came and Mom told them they needn't
come back again.

We went to Oolitic again on Saturday. Dad said the
car was knocking and needed work done on it. He said
he'd bet that Troy Michaels hadn't had that car serviced

within the past year. And if he didn't see to it now, it wouldn't last another one. So we all piled into the car and rode into town with him.

The car did make some racket. I heard a lot of new noises that hadn't been there the week before, but we made it up and down the hills without any trouble. When Dad let us out of the car in front of the Rainbow Store, Johnny and Byron were waiting there with Linzy Meaders as if they knew we were coming but just didn't know when to expect us.

Mom said that she and Linzy were going to the bank before they did their trading and handed me a fifty-cent piece.

"Seely, take this and get a soda for everyone."

Linzy said, "The boys have money. Gus has been paying them thirty-five cents a day to help him at the sawmill this past week."

So that's why they haven't been to our house, I thought. They weren't afraid of Schylar and Sylvester. They were busy working at the mill.

"It's my kids' turn to buy," Mom told Linzy. "Seely will pay for the sodas."

With that, they turned down the street toward the bank and left us to go the other way to the drug store. As they were leaving, I heard Mom say, "I've had my heart set on one of those treadle machines. And I figure if I can put a little money aside each week, by fall I'll have enough saved to get one."

I knew that Mom wanted a sewing machine. I had heard her say so many times. But I thought her wish for a machine to do her patching and mending was like my want for a big dictionary so I could learn about words—an unattainable thing in my mind, and so far out of reach that it was foolish to even think of it.

At the drug store, we sat at the same table we'd had the week before, ordered sodas, and watched the people who passed by on the street. But this Saturday we didn't see the now familiar faces of the Fender twins outside the window. And as I told Johnny, after seeing them every day from daylight to dark, I was not eager to see them again soon.

Johnny and Byron laughed.

"Your ma must have taken all the starch out of their tails," Johnny said, still laughing. "We haven't seen Schylar and Sylvester skulking through the woods or sneaking along the path behind us since the day she took them in hand."

We finished our sodas, and when I paid the bill I got a dime back from the fifty-cent piece that Mom had given me. I didn't have a pocket, so I let Robert carry the change. I knew he wouldn't lose it. He was too proud that I trusted him with the money to be careless with it.

Outside the door, Johnny turned in the opposite direction from the way we had come and took us back to the Rainbow Store by a different street.

"We'll show you the town," he said. "Then you won't get lost here." After a moment, he added with a grin, "That's just in case I'm not here to look after you all the time."

I paid close attention to every turn and street crossing until I recognized the old junk store ahead of us. Then I knew where we were. Oolitic wasn't so big, I thought.

I could lose my way twice in the same day and still find the Rainbow Store before Mom even missed me.

Johnny and Byron stayed with Robert and me until we found Mom and Linzy. Then they left us to do whatever had brought them to town in the first place.

Linzy said the boys had probably gone to the garage. They usually spent every Saturday down there watching the men work on cars. "Those two never seem to get their fill of looking at automobiles or messing around with the engines," she said.

I told Linzy that I hadn't thought they came to town to drink a soda with Robert and me. She just smiled and went on with her shopping.

Mom and Linzy took their own sweet time about filling their baskets, but we still had quite a wait before Dad drove up and stopped in front of the store. If we hadn't been looking for the car we never would have heard it. All the knocks and noises had been taken out and the motor ran with a soft, smooth hum.

Mom went to the Shiloh Baptist Church for prayer meeting with Fanny Phillips that Sunday evening. Dad remarked that he couldn't see a dime's worth of difference between the revival in Jubilee and the prayer meeting in Shiloh, since neither one was Methodist. But if Mom had her heart set on going, he wouldn't stand in her way.

Mom replied that it so happened she did and got in the car with Fanny and roared away over the hill. Dad shook his head and said, to himself mostly, "The way that woman drives, a body would have to be almighty hard up for somewhere to go to ever get in an automobile with her."

I didn't mention that Mom was used to that kind of driving, and a few minutes later I was glad I hadn't. The dust hadn't settled on the road behind Fanny Phillips' car when Johnny Meaders and Byron Tyson appeared at our back door.

"Ma was wondering could the kids go to the revival with us," Johnny said, when Dad asked them into the house. "We'd bring them home afterwards," he added as further persuasion.

Dad said it was up to me. But if I went, I'd have to take Robert. Without hesitation, I said yes. Even though it meant I had to take Robert with me, I wanted to go. I knew that Mom wouldn't approve of our going to Jubilee, but she would have to go through Dad to raise Cain with me. He had practically given me his permission to go.

Linzy and Ednalice were waiting where the woods path met the wagon road. Linzy said that Grandma Stoner was ailing, so she had brought Ednalice along to keep her from disturbing the old woman. She laughed when I told her I had brought Robert because Mom wasn't home. She had gone to the Baptist church with Fanny Phillips.

"I'd wager my bottom dollar that Zel sits through that sermon," Linzy said with a chuckle. "It would be too infernally far from home for her to walk out on Pastor Wolfe."

I guess the thought amused Linzy. Every so often she would laugh softly at nothing at all, and once she remarked that Zel would probably find that one visit to Shiloh with Fanny would be one time too many, also.

Ednalice was three years older than Robert, but she started mothering him as if she was three times his age. They skipped ahead of the rest of us, stopping now and then to study a strange flowering weed that had taken Robert's eye.

But they never lingered long enough for us to catch up to them. Ednalice would bend her brown head to touch Robert's honey-blond one and listen quietly to his every word. Then she would toss her head back and laugh, her fine long hair flying every which way about her face. Whenever she caught a glimpse of her mother or the boys and me gaining on them, she would whisper to Robert, take his hand, and run out of reach.

Linzy smiled at the picture Ednalice and Robert made, running and laughing in the twilight. "Now, ain't that a sight?" she said softly, never taking her eyes off them for a minute.

I was glad to know that Linzy was watching the kids. That meant I could walk with Johnny and Byron and not have to wonder about what Robert was doing. I could give all my attention to what the boys were saying to me.

When we passed the Fender house Linzy glanced at the dim-lit windows, but she didn't comment on Nellie being at home nor make any move toward the house. I thought she would probably ask Nellie to go to the revival with us. She always did. But tonight she didn't mention it. And I felt that it wasn't my place to say anything about it.

123

We got to the schoolhouse early. Johnny and Byron left us and went to talk to a group of boys who were standing off to one side of the building. Linzy took the kids and me inside. Someone had lit the lanterns and hung them around the room, but there were only a few of the older members seated at the front of the room. Most of the people were scattered around outside talking.

I supposed aloud that they were waiting like Johnny and Byron for full dark before they came in and sat down. But Linzy said they were waiting for the preacher to get there. Mister Paully didn't always get here on time, Linzy explained. He drove a huckster wagon for Ab Griffin during the week, selling to the folks back in the hills. And when he had to stock the wagon on Sunday, he was late for prayer meeting.

"Preaching the gospel is Mister Paully's calling," Linzy said, leading the way to a front pew. "But selling is his living. Preaching don't pay nothing," she added under her breath.

We had just settled ourselves in the seat when the Reverend Mister Paully came down the aisle and stepped to the desk in the center of the platform. As he opened his Bible, his long hands covering the spread pages, the people stopped whispering and fanning themselves and gave him their undivided attention.

I did too. I looked the preacher up and down, from head to foot. Up close, I could tell that his black coat and trousers didn't match, and both were in dire need of pressing with a damp cloth and a hot flat iron, and his shoes were worn and cracked across the toes.

I raised my eyes to study the preacher's face. The

fiery zeal and spirit of the past Sunday were missing from his coal-black eyes. They seemed almost placid and lent a kindliness to the rest of his face. I wondered why I had ever found him a strange and frightening figure.

At one time during the sermon, the Reverend Mister Paully had it going hot and heavy. But then the enthusiasm seemed to cool down, and the prayer meeting was over before he got it well off the ground. The men and women who had been dancing in the aisles and shouting hallelujah loud enough to be heard in heaven turned and filed quietly out the door. The Reverend Paully was left standing there, spent and alone on the platform that served as his pulpit.

Linzy whispered that she guessed the preacher was too tired to breathe the fire of life into the gathering tonight and stood up, preparing to leave the room. But since we were seated in a front pew, we were the last ones to get to the door and into the cool night air.

There was a full moon over the tree tops, and it seemed lighter outside than it had been in the church. Mothers called their children, and when they were all together families moved in all directions for home.

Linzy held on to Ednalice. Ednalice held Robert's hand. And I looked around for Johnny and Byron to walk with me. I hadn't seen the boys since they had left us before the meeting started, and I didn't find them now. We had passed the general store and left it far behind when they finally caught up with us.

"The fellows at prayer meeting said they had heard that the Fender boys were going to be laying for me tonight," Johnny said, when Linzy asked what had kept them. "Byron and me thought we'd hang back a-ways and if Schylar and Sylvester had it in mind to start trouble, we'd be ready for them. But nothing happened," he added.

"You're not home yet," Linzy said dryly.

Johnny and Byron laughed, then took the stones they had in their pockets and threw them at the telephone poles along the road.

After that, Linzy led the singing, and we sang one song after another. The ones that I didn't know, I listened to the tune, then hummed the chorus that came after every two or three lines of words. By the time we got to the wagon road that led to the Meaders' place, I think we had all forgotten the Fender boys and their threat to Johnny. I know I had.

Linzy and Ednalice turned on the lane, but instead of us going part way with them, then cutting through the woods like Robert wanted to do, we followed the pike road down the hill and past the old truck. Seen by moonlight, I thought the truck looked like a pile of junk and wished out loud that they would come and haul it away.

Johnny laughed. "It'll get hauled away," he said. "But it will be taken a piece at a time."

The words were barely out of his mouth when rocks began to pelt the ground around us like hailstones.

Byron yelled, "You kids get down!" He grabbed Robert and pushed him into the deep side ditch.

I stood beside the road like an idiot, my arms crossed over my head and rocks falling all around me. Johnny shoved me hard toward the ditch. "And stay there!" he told me.

126

I crouched on my hands and knees in the ditch for what seemed like hours, shielding Robert from the flying stones and thinking they would never stop.

I wondered where Johnny and Byron had taken shelter and what they were doing. Rocks rattled off the side of the old truck and I heard Byron yell, "Hey! You missed us again!" and I knew then that the boys were deliberately drawing attention to their hiding place and away from Robert and me.

As the stones continued to come thick and fast from the trees, I thought to myself that the Fender boys must have gathered every loose stone on the road between Jubilee and the White River bridge and stored them for just such a time as this one. There were huge boulders among the trees, but small stones do not grow plentiful in the woods.

The attack stopped as suddenly as it had begun, and everything was quiet. I held my breath and listened, but I couldn't hear a sound from the woods. They've finally run out of rocks, I thought, and stood up, making a perfect target in the moonlight. A stone came whistling out of the trees, struck me on the forehead, and I fell flat on the ground.

I must have been hit by the last stone thrown by either side. It wasn't long afterwards that Johnny called that we could come out now. The Fenders were gone.

"I heard them running toward town as if their tails were on fire," Johnny said, as he helped me to my feet. Then he saw the blood on my face and turned to call Byron. "Seely's been hit!"

"Damn them to hell," he said, as he pulled a wadded

handkerchief from his pocket to wipe my face. "It's almost clean," Johnny told me. "I've only used it a couple of days."

Mom would've had a conniption fit at the very thought of Johnny putting a dirty rag over an open cut, I thought. Even if she knew it was to keep me from bleeding to death!

Which I wasn't. Byron said it looked like the stone had just grazed me in passing. "If you'd have stayed put like we told you . . ."

Robert said, "Damn them to hell. They hit Seely with a rock."

For just a second, it was so quiet that we could have heard the leaves float to the ground. Then Byron took Robert by the shoulders and gave him a shaking. "Don't you ever say damn and hell again," he told Robert. "If your ma ever hears you cussing like a coal miner, you'll never get to go to church with Ednalice again."

Byron took Robert by the hand and hurried him down the road toward home, leaving Johnny and me to walk together.

Johnny said, "Byron's right, you know. After what's happened here tonight, your ma may never allow you to go any place with me ever again."

I had the same thought in mind. But I told Johnny that I couldn't see how Mom could blame them for the rock fight. They hadn't started it. And besides that, he and Byron had done all they could to keep Robert and me safe from harm.

"Mom likes you and Byron," I said. "So does Dad.

They wouldn't be nearly as apt to blame you as they would to say it was my own fault. I shouldn't have got out where the Fender boys could see me," I added.

Fanny Phillips had brought Mom home and left before Johnny and I got to the house. But Byron and Robert were there first and told Mom about the rock fight with the Fenders, and she was waiting with the turpentine and Clover Leaf salve to take care of the cut on my forehead.

"You could've lost the sight in that eye," Mom said, as she doused the cut with turpentine, then smeared salve over it and tied a clean strip of cotton around my head. "If that stone had struck a quarter of an inch lower, you'd have been blind as a bat in one eye," she added.

"But if it had been a couple of inches higher," I said, "it would've missed me completely."

She smacked me lightly on the back of the head, and said it was my own fault that I was hit at all. I should have minded what the boys told me.

While Mom was busy tending to my head, Dad had been talking to Johnny and Byron on the back porch. I don't know what they told Dad about the stoning, but as Mom was putting the salve and bandages away, he came into the kitchen, took a stick of stove wood from the woodbox and hefted it in his hand, as if testing its weight or staying power. Or both.

"I'm going to walk a-ways with the boys," he told Mom, his face dark and angry in the lamplight. "Lock the door behind me and go on to bed. I may be a while."

129

He paused with his hand on the door knob and turned to face her. "Don't leave a light burning. Far as anyone else need know, we've all gone to bed."

Mom didn't say a word as he closed the door and left, carrying the stick of stove wood with him.

Mom bolted the door, then picked up the lamp to light our way to bed. She didn't mention her evening with Fanny Phillips or the Shiloh Baptist Church. But she did say that if she had been at home, Robert and I wouldn't have been allowed to go to Jubilee with Johnny and Byron.

"And what's more," she said, "if you had minded my words about those Holy Rollers, you wouldn't have been on that road when the Fender boys jumped Johnny Meaders tonight."

Mom turned back Robert's bed and wouldn't look at me as she went on. "Then your daddy wouldn't be out there now, with fire in his eyes and a club in his hand, just itching for the chance to use it."

She set the lamp on the chest, blew out the light, and left the room. A few minutes later, I heard the springs squeak as she settled herself in her bed. I knew she wouldn't sleep until Dad got home and she had satisfied herself that he was all right.

I didn't think I could sleep either. But I did. My last conscious thought was of the white fear on Mom's face when Dad left the house, and the angry red flush on his face as he hefted the chunk of wood. I wondered if all our emotions wore a certain color. And if they did, what would be the color of carefree joy and pleasure. I couldn't remember ever seeing either one of these on Mom or Dad's face.

The sound of the door opening and closing as Mom let Dad back into the house woke me. I heard a dull thud as the stove wood landed in the woodbox. Then Dad said, "Those Fender boys must sleep during the day and roam the country all night. I went straight to Nellie Fender. I aimed to have it out with them, once and for all time. But she took me in and showed me—Schylar and Sylvester weren't sleeping in their bed at home."

Dad's steps crossed the room, and my bedroom door was closed quietly. I couldn't hear what else was being said. Mom let our bedroom door swing wide open when Dad was away, but I guess he couldn't stand the sight of our open door. He always made sure it was shut tight before he went to bed.

I thought to myself, "I'll ask Mom in the morning what went on out there tonight," and went sound asleep again.

chapter sixteen

*T*he very first thing the next morning, Linzy Meaders came knocking at our back door. She asked Mom if I had been hurt bad when the Fenders stoned Johnny and Byron and said she was more than sorry that it had happened the one time Robert and I had walked home with the boys.

Mom sniffed and sloughed it off as nothing at all. "I've seen worse scratches from a blackberry briar," she said.

She didn't mention that Dad had thought the stoning serious enough to go after the ones who had done it with a stick of stove wood.

"This ain't the first time it's happened," Linzy said. "But I never thought much about it before. The boys seem to expect some kind of trap or deadfall of the Fender twins every time they leave the house. I think they even look forward to besting Schylar and Sylvester at their own game. But now, it's gone too far, gotten out of hand, I'd say."

She hesitated, as if she wasn't quite sure whether or not to say what she had on her mind or how Mom would take her words.

"Nellie was warned years ago that her boys could be dangerous and she ought to do something about them. But she wouldn't do nothing. One of these days," Linzy said gravely, "Schylar and Sylvester will hurt someone real bad. And then it will be too late to do anything after the harm is done."

Mom didn't seem to take Linzy's words too seriously. She smiled and touched her shoulder as she went to the stove for the bubbling coffee pot.

"Nellie Fender seems to be able to handle her boys pretty well without our help," Mom said. "And I'll grant them this much, they didn't give me any sass or cause any trouble over here." Then she laughed, and added quickly, "But I wouldn't ask for another week alone with those two boys."

She poured two cups of coffee, placed one in front of Linzy, then sat down at the table with her.

"I didn't come over the hill to talk about the Fenders," Linzy said, drawing the coffee cup nearer to her. "It's Grandma Stoner that I'm concerned about. She hasn't been feeling a bit good lately."

When Mom asked what seemed to be her trouble,

Linzy replied that she thought it was the summer complaint. "I know it's early in the season," she said, "but that's what I'd say was ailing her."

Linzy blew on her coffee to cool it, then took a cautious sip. "What beats me," she said, "ever since the word got out that Grandma was feeling poorly, the house has been overrun with folks coming in to see her." She shook her head slowly, as if puzzled by the way of human nature, then went on. "They can live all their lives within hollering distance of one another and never take the time to stop and say how are you. But let one of the old ones take sick, and they'll flock in like a gaggle of geese, as if this will be their last chance to ever lay eyes on them."

I saw the shadow of a remembered sorrow cross Mom's face, but it was gone with the blink of an eye. "Is there anything I can do to help?" Mom asked.

"There may be." Linzy thanked Mom with a smile. "It's got to the point where Grandma can't help herself. Why, if she took a notion for a cup of tea, she couldn't boil the water."

Mom looked at me, her eyes searching my face as if she expected to find there the answer to a question that only she knew. Then she turned to Linzy and said, "I can let you take Seely for a few days, if you could use her."

I couldn't believe that I had heard Mom right. Just last summer she had hesitated to loan me to Clara Brent for a day. And here she was offering me to Linzy Meaders as if I was a gunny sack full of puny potatoes. And as far as I could tell, not giving a second thought to how

I would fare in the deal. I thought to myself, "Mom sure has changed!"

"That's what I had in mind to ask you." Linzy's words broke my line of thought, and I sat up and paid attention to see what I was getting into here.

"If Seely could come over for a few hours a day, I'd appreciate it," Linzy said. "Having her there with Grandma would be a blessing. And I'd feel free to leave the house once in a while," she added.

She turned to me as she got up from the table. "Seely, if you'd rather not be saddled with Grandma for the summer, just say so. I'll understand."

I saw the look on Mom's face and it was my turn to understand. For the first time in my life, Mom was treating me like a grownup and hoping that I wouldn't disappoint her but that I would act like one.

"I've never had any dealings with old people," I told Linzy. "But if Grandma Stoner doesn't mind my ignorance, I'm sure not afraid to try doing for her."

Mom and Linzy smiled at each other, and I could almost swear that Mom sighed with relief.

Linzy said that today would be as good a time as any for me to get acquainted with Grandma and motioned for me to follow her from the kitchen. Mom walked as far as the porch steps with us, reminding me to behave myself and do as Linzy told me.

At the foot of the steps, Linzy stopped and turned back to face Mom. "Zel, with all that I've got on my mind, I near forgot to ask: how did you like the Shiloh Baptist service?"

I think Linzy deliberately waited on purpose to ask

that when we were leaving the house. She spoke offhand, as if it was of no importance to her, one way or another. But I noticed that she stood still and waited for Mom to answer.

"I can't say that I liked or disliked the Baptist service," Mom replied. "In a way, it was as different from the Methodist prayer meetings as the Holy Roller revival." She flushed a deep red and smiled with embarrassment and shame. "It was my first experience with the Holy Roller services," she said. "And it took me by surprise."

Linzy didn't say anything, but her face had a waiting look about it, as if there was something more that she wanted to hear from Mom.

"I've been thinking," Mom said quietly, "that since the young'uns get along so well together and seem bound and determined to go to the Holy Roller revival that I'd walk along with you next Sunday and try it again. That is," she added, "if you all will have me."

Linzy smiled all over and waved her hand. "You're welcome, Zel," she said.

chapter seventeen

I had never been inside the Meaders' house, and when I followed Linzy in from the bright sunlight, the room seemed dark and gloomy. I stopped just inside the door and waited for my eyes to adjust to the strange dimness, then moved further into the room.

Grandma Stoner was sitting at the kitchen table and didn't even look up when we walked in or act like she knew there was anyone else in the room. She was busily soaking bread in a cup of coffee, then sucking the soggy mess through her toothless gums. She made a horrible noise, but I noticed that she didn't once miss her mouth or even dribble coffee on the table cloth.

Linzy put her hand on the old woman's shoulder and

said, "Grandma, I've brought someone to keep you company."

Grandma Stoner's beady-bright old eyes lit on me, and I knew at once that she had known I was there all the time. She had just been waiting and taking my measure, watching like an ancient cat at a mouse hole to see which way I would run.

I felt like running, but I held my ground and smiled as I stepped nearer to the table and the old woman.

She licked her fingers with the tip of her tongue, then put out her hand to shake hands with me. I had dreaded the moment when I would have to touch her. She looked so dried-out and fragile that I thought she would feel crackly like old leather. But her hand was soft and just as smooth and warm as a new flannel nightgown.

When she gave my hand a slight tug, I squatted on my heels so my face would be on a level with hers. She seemed to be smiling, but with so many wrinkles and lines running across her face, I couldn't be sure. I felt her hand touch my head gently for a moment. Then she said, "Towhead! A towheaded gal!" and smacked my shoulder with more strength than I would have thought possible from one of her years.

I laughed out loud and leaned farther back on my heels to take a better look at Grandma Stoner.

"Don't you like towheaded girls?" I asked her.

She said, "Humph!" which could have meant anything, and went back to her bread and coffee.

After telling Ednalice to mind what I told her and give a hand with Grandma, Linzy said she had business to tend to and left the house. She hadn't said what I was supposed to do while she was away.

I sat down across the table from Grandma Stoner and watched as her head bent to meet her fingers every time they left the cup. Her back and shoulders were so rounded and humped that there was hardly any distance between her face and the table. Yet she made the motion, anyhow.

"What're you staring at, gal?"

I had been so intent on watching her and wondering how many years it had taken for her to get so wrinkled and bent that her voice startled me. I couldn't say a word.

"Well? What's the matter? Cat got your tongue?"

Her words came at me too fast for me to think. I spoke what was on my mind.

I said, "How old are you?"

She pushed her cup to the middle of the table and got up. "That's none of your business," she said. But I knew she was smiling when she said it. Her beady black eyes were sparkling.

Grandma Stoner let me wash her face and hands, and when I told her she might have company today, she stood still while I changed the soiled wrapper she wore for a clean cotton dress Linzy had laid out for her. When I went to get the comb and brush, Ednalice said that Grandma would raise a fuss and hit me with the brush if I tried to comb her hair. "She won't allow Ma or me to touch it," she said.

I told Ednalice to go outside and play. I would tend to Grandma Stoner.

"Don't say I didn't warn you," she whispered as she left the room.

I picked up the comb and brush from the dresser and went back to the kitchen where I had left Grandma. She had seemed docile enough so far, but what Ednalice had said made me a little bit leery of her. I didn't want to make the old woman mad at me, but her hair sorely needed care. And I aimed to see that she got it.

Grandma was moving toward the front door, her feet not leaving the floor, but slipping slowly one after the other across the linoleum.

"Would you like to sit on the porch?" I put my hand on her arm, but she shrugged it off.

"I don't need any help to find my rocking chair," she said.

So I held the door open for her.

She shuffled to her chair, sat down, then rested her head on the chair back, closing her eyes against the brightness of the day and letting the sun warm her.

Ednalice was peddling around the yard on a battered cast-iron tricycle. She stopped peddling long enough to give me a sly wink and an I-told-you-so smile, then whirled away again.

I waited a moment longer, then stepped behind the rocker and began gently to remove the pins from the old woman's hair.

"What're you doing, now?" Grandma Stoner sounded cross and ill-tempered, but she didn't pull away or tell me to stop and leave her alone.

"You'll rest better without these pins," I said softly, and kept right on loosening her hair.

I put the pins in my pocket and ran my fingers through the tight roll of hair, separating the strands and letting her get used to the touch of my hands. Then I started at the end of each strand and gently brushed away the tangles, speaking softly all the while and asking questions to keep her mind on other things. When I got it all untangled, Grandma had soft, baby-fine hair that lay smooth and close to her head. But it had a sour smell as if it could stand a good soaping.

I wouldn't try that today, I thought. I considered myself mighty lucky to get it combed and brushed without a big fuss.

I leaned over the chair to see why she was being so quiet. Grandma Stoner was sound asleep. I brushed for a moment longer, then left her to finish her nap. But I promised myself that one day soon I would shampoo Grandma's hair and maybe even talk her into taking a bath all over.

I decided that while Grandma was asleep, I would make her bed. And I would do it smooth and neat, the way Clara Brent had taught me to make a bed. Then if Grandma wanted to lie down for a while later, it would be all ready for her.

I was almost to the door when I heard her old voice saying real soft and low, "I was a towheaded gal when I was a young'un."

I smiled at her slyness. Grandma Stoner hadn't been sleeping as soundly as I had thought.

The time at the Meaders' place passed as swiftly as a cool breeze on a hot day and left the same good feeling when it was gone. I ran and skipped all the way home.

I liked Grandma. She wasn't any trouble at all. But tomorrow, I thought, I'll take Robert along to play with Ednalice. Then I can spend all my time talking with Grandma Stoner.

Mom was bringing in the last of the washing off the line when I got home. I took an armload and talked about my day at the Meaders' while we sorted clothes and put them away.

"Linzy says that Grandma likes me, that I did fine."

Mom said, "Never figured otherwise." And left the room to set our supper on the table.

We had bean soup. And as I ate my fair share, I thought to myself, "Julie's right, as usual. The beans do have a slight flavor of Fels-Naptha soap and bluing." But I kept my mouth shut. It had been too good a day to spoil it now.

chapter eighteen

On my way home from the Meaders' the next day, I met Nellie Fender. She said she had been waiting for me. "My boys, they didn't aim to hit you," she said, in her halting way of speaking.

I took a good look around us to make sure Schylar and Sylvester weren't hiding in the trees and thought to myself, They couldn't have hit truer if they had been aiming. But I told Nellie that they hadn't hurt me. "The stone just grazed my head as it went by," I said.

Robert and I started on down the path, and Nellie turned and matched her steps to ours. She kept pace with us all the way through the woods and only stopped when our house came in sight on the dirt road.

"Come and say how are you to Mom," I said, as she hesitated at the edge of the road.

She shook her head. "Just thought to see you safe home," she said, stumbling over her words. "I didn't know you'd have the boy with you."

Nellie turned back the way we had come, and a moment later she disappeared among the trees.

I guess I had been going to the Meaders' house to look after Grandma Stoner for more than a week when I realized that someone was following me through the woods. I never heard anything except his chatter on the days that Robert went with me. But when I went alone, I was almost positive that I wasn't ever really alone on the path. That not far behind me, there were others treading this same trail and making sure that I didn't see them.

At first, I thought it was just my imagination. The wooded hills and hollows were still strange to me, and I told myself that the sounds I heard could be the creakings of an old tree, or dead branches rubbing together and the dried limbs breaking. Even wild creatures scurrying through the underbrush could make the sounds that I heard day after day. But I didn't really think so.

Then one afternoon I caught the whisper of voices coming from somewhere in front of me. I couldn't see anyone, and probably wouldn't have thought a thing about it had they spoken out loud as one would do naturally. But these were furtive, suppressed words, ending in soft snickering laughter.

I knew then that it was the Fender twins on the path

ahead of me. No one else laughed the way they did. I figured they had been the ones who were following me all the time. They must feel pretty sure of themselves today, I thought. They had been sneaking and stalking me for a week, and this was the first time they had been brave enough to come out where I could recognize them.

I slipped quietly off the path, intending to hide in a nearby hazelnut thicket or sassafras patch until they had gone on by me, but when I left the familiar path behind me, I lost all sense of direction. Once I thought I heard them slipping through the brush behind me. I dropped to the ground and kept my head low as I crept farther into the thickets and away from the path toward home.

I held my breath and listened. When I didn't hear a thing except my heart beating, I stood up and ran aimlessly through the young sassafras and paw-paw trees to get as far away as possible from where I had last heard Schylar and Sylvester Fender, and where I suspected they were still looking for me. By luck, I came to the secret cove hidden in the hillside. Here was a safe haven. I fell full length on the soft grassy floor of the cove to rest and catch my breath.

I don't know how long I lay there before the complete stillness of the woods told me I was alone. If the Fender twins had been following me, I had lost them somewhere along the way.

I sat up and looked around me. I knew this shady glen and cove, but I wasn't sure of the way Robert and I had turned when we left it. I got to my feet, facing the high arch of trees overhead, and walked backwards, much the same as Robert and I had done the day we found the cove, and so I found my way out of the woods to the dirt road that would lead me home.

I kept a close watch along the way, but I didn't see any sign of Schylar and Sylvester Fender. But that didn't mean they hadn't been there before me, I thought.

Mom didn't question the lateness of the hour. Since I had been helping out at the Meaders' house, I was apt to get home any time of the day. Sometimes, Linzy wouldn't need me for more than an hour or two. Then on other days, I would be there from early morning until late in the afternoon.

chapter nineteen

I had thought that I would see a lot of Johnny and Byron while I was taking care of Grandma Stoner. It was their custom to stay with Linzy all week while Jack was away, then go to Aunt Fanny's in Jubilee for Saturday and Sunday. But I found that they were usually just leaving the house or had already gone when I got there in the morning. And I would have to leave before they got home in the afternoon.

One day I asked Linzy where the boys had been keeping themselves. "I never see them except in Oolitic on Saturday," I said.

They were either helping Gus at the sawmill or off on some matter of their own, she answered. "Who knows what boys are up to nowadays?"

I said I didn't. That was for sure!

But I could be sure of one thing. Recently, whenever I had gone alone to the Meaders' house, somewhere along the path in the woods, I could expect to find Nellie Fender waiting to walk home with me. I never knew where she would be, and she gave no reason for being there, yet she would suddenly step out of the trees ahead of me and wait patiently until I got to her.

At first, the hesitation between her words bothered me. It was all I could do to keep from saying the words for her. But as time went on, I found Nellie's stuttering to be kind of restful. The pauses gave me time to study Nellie, and by listening really close I could tell what she was saying.

It was the last of June, and Grandma Stoner had been irritable and as unruly as a child all day. I couldn't really blame Grandma for her crankiness. She had broken out with a heat rash beneath her bosom, and she was galled raw where her legs rubbed together up near her straddle. I knew she had to be uncomfortable. And I did everything I could think of to make her feel better.

I gave Grandma a cool sponge bath and powered the rash the way she had told me to do with soda and burnt flour. Then I put fresh underwear and a clean cotton wrapper on her. While she was eating her breakfast of biscuits and cold tea, I changed her bed. I figured that with clean sheets pulled smooth and tight and the window blinds drawn to shut out the sun, Grandma might be able to sleep awhile before the day got too unbearably hot.

Grandma Stoner did sleep for a time. But she woke up

just as irritable. I couldn't do a thing to suit her. I told Linzy that I hoped July, which was just a turn of the calendar page away, wouldn't be so hot and muggy. Then maybe Grandma's rash would go away and she'd stop complaining.

Linzy said I shouldn't let her bother me. Grandma always got cranky in hot weather. I knew Grandma Stoner had good reason to be cranky, and I was sorry for her. But I was still glad when it came time for me to leave the Meaders' house and go home.

I hurried across the field toward the welcome shade of the trees. I couldn't count on finding a breeze in the woods when the day was hot and still like this one, but the shade made it seem cooler under the trees. Before I was halfway to the woods, sweat had soaked my shirt and it clung to me like a second skin. It didn't do any good to pull it loose and shake it. After a few steps the blouse would be stuck to me just as tight as ever.

Nellie was waiting in the shade at the edge of the woods and didn't take her eyes off me as I raised my blouse and fanned it up and down to dry the sweat and cool myself.

"I wasn't much bigger than you are now," Nellie said, "the day my uncle Emery found me alone, took me, and got me in the family way."

She had never spoken to me like this before, and coming as it did after the hectic day I had had at the Meaders', it baffled me. I dropped my shirttail and took a step back to look at her. Nellie's face was naturally rosy, and the sun and heat heightened her color. But now she was flushed a deep red.

I thought to myself, "This is Nellie's way of telling me about having Schylar and Sylvester."

I cleared my mind and prepared to pay close attention to whatever else she had to tell me. I was surprised when she didn't mention their names, but it seemed to me that it wasn't the twins or herself that concerned Nellie today. It was me.

She said, "You look like a woman, but you ain't yet. Not by a long sight."

Nellie raised her head, and her eyes searched my face. "You understand my meaning, don't you, Seely?"

I nodded without speaking.

"You're still a young'un" she said gently. "And you want a lot of growing before that happens."

I wondered what ailed Nellie today. She talked like her brain had been addled by the heat. She ought to know without my saying so that I wouldn't allow anyone to touch me. But I told her, anyhow, that if she meant what I thought she meant, THAT was never going to happen to me. No matter how much growing I did!

I started to move on down the path, but Nellie put out her hand and stopped me. Then she just stood waiting, as if there was more she wanted to say, but she couldn't seem to get the words to come out.

I said, "Nellie, are you trying to tell me that you're afraid someone will do to me what your uncle Emery did to you?"

She nodded. "And care not one whit for the damage they do you," she said without stuttering.

I smiled at Nellie to let her know I understood and

appreciated her concern. But her worry was wasted, I told her.

"No harm can come to me," I said, wanting to put her mind at ease. "Mom watches me like a hawk when I'm at home, and I've got you to see that I get there safely. Besides," I added, "I can outrun any man in these parts."

Nellie said I shouldn't make light of her warning. She just wanted to put me on my guard for a time when one of them wouldn't be near about.

"No doubt you'd be safe enough at the Meaders' place, and between there and home," she said. "But then, you can't be too careful at your age."

I wondered again what had happened to upset Nellie. She had lived for seventeen years with what her uncle Emery had done to her. It couldn't be that, not after all this time. From the way she talked, I figured it must have been something she had heard concerning me. Probably some careless remark that Nellie had heard someone say and taken it to mean a threat to my well-being, I thought. And I went on down the path toward home.

Nellie said she had lived here all her life and knew the country like the back of her hand. But this afternoon, she scanned the hills and hollows as if it was all strange territory and if she didn't watch her step she would get lost and not be able to find her way home.

I said good-bye to Nellie at the top of the ridge and went down the hill to the house. But when I turned in at our gate, I glanced back at the ridge and Nellie was still there.

Mom knew that Nellie Fender sometimes walked me

home and hardly ever commented on it other than to ask, "What did Nellie have to say?" But today Mom was sitting on the front porch fanning herself and didn't even say hey as I went by her and into the house. And the fan didn't miss a lick, either.

I would have been hard put to find the words to tell Mom the things that Nellie had to say today. There were some things I could tell her, but a lot more that I didn't dare to talk about. And Nellie's warning, if that's what it was, came under the heading of the things I didn't tell Mom.

In the first place, Mom wouldn't approve of the things Nellie had told me about her uncle Emery, and she might forbid me ever to speak to her again. And if Mom ever got wind of a threat of danger to me, she would put a stop to my helping Linzy with Grandma Stoner. Trying as the old woman could be at times, I wasn't ready to give up the two dollars that Linzy gave me every Saturday for putting up with her. So I kept my mouth shut and my eyes open and went right on doing the same as I had all summer.

chapter twenty

I didn't see much of Johnny and Byron during the week, but we still met in Oolitic on Saturday. We would have a cold soda at the drug store, then walk around town looking in the store windows and wishing, while Mom and Linzy went to the bank and did their trading at the Rainbow Store. Then on Saturday night, Johnny would bring his guitar to our house as he'd been doing for sometime now, and we would all sit on the back porch and sing while he played the music.

We went to the prayer meeting at the Jubilee school-house, but Johnny and Byron wouldn't walk with us. They had heard some threats that Schylar and Sylvester Fender had made against them, and they were afraid one of us might get hurt again. I thought the boys were being foolish. Even they ought to know by now that the Fenders weren't about to start a fracas or throw stones as long as Mom was walking with us. If they bothered Mom, she would find enough work to keep Schylar and Sylvester busy for the rest of the summer.

When I got to Meaders' house on Monday morning, Linzy was chopping stove wood, laying the axe to the block as if it was to blame for all her trouble.

"I thought Johnny kept the woodbox filled," I said, as a way of greeting her.

"Since those two boys have been working for Gus at the sawmill, I never get a lick of help." She set another chunk of wood on end and split it in half with one blow from the axe. "He's either frittering away his time on that guitar or swimming in the blue hole."

As hot as it was this morning, I told Linzy, a swim in anything would feel good. "But what's a blue hole?"

"A quarry hole that has filled with water," Linzy answered. "And you stay away from it. That's no place for a girl." She stooped to gather an armload of wood to carry into the house. "It's dangerous for the boys, and I've warned them against it, but they will slip off and swim there, anyway."

Suddenly there was a rattle of pots and pans from the kitchen and the sound of Grandma Stoner quarreling to herself. She was ready for her morning coffee, I heard her mutter, and the cook stove was stone cold!

I hurried on to the house, and from the moment I stepped through the kitchen door until she went to her rocker after lunch, Grandma kept me hopping to wait on her hand and foot. Linzy said that I humored her too much, that I spoiled her. "She'll wear you out, if you let her," Linzy said.

"Grandma is no bother," I said, and crossed my fingers. "She just wants a little attention." I smiled at Linzy, and added, "Besides, that's what I get paid to do."

Linzy shook her head and turned away, as if to say she had washed her hands of the both of us, Grandma and me.

When we had finished our noon meal, the kitchen was like a bake oven. We stacked the dishes and went to the front porch, hoping to find a cool breeze. The big tree that stood near the corner of the house shaded that one whole side, and if there was a breeze anywhere, we would find it there.

Ednalice swayed slowly back and forth in the old rubber tire swing, while the dog lay at her feet and let the sweat drip off the end of his tongue, too lazy, Linzy said, to even move out of the child's way.

Grandma Stoner dozed off and on in the rocking chair, then slept soundly with her mouth open and her chin resting on her thin chest.

"I don't know how she can sleep in this heat," Linzy said. She tossed the cardboard fan she carried to one side and sat down beside me on the porch steps. "It's too infernally hot to even stir the air," she said. Then she added, "Or to do much of anything else, either."

I thought of the cool, shady path through the woods and the cold well water from the pump at home. "Then if you think you won't need me," I said, "I'd like to go home."

Linzy sat with her elbows on her knees and her face cupped in the palms of her hands, just resting. "You might as well," she said quietly. "I don't intend to move from this spot until the day cools a bit."

As I stood up to leave, the thought came to me that Nellie Fender wouldn't be waiting this early in the afternoon. She would never expect me until much later in the day, because for some time now I'd been staying at the Meaders' until late afternoon. And with the thought of Nellie, all the things she had warned me about came rushing to the front of my mind.

She was trying to look after me, I thought. But who had ever cared and tended for Nellie? She had never married. Or had she, and I just didn't know about it?

"Whatever happened to Nellie Fender's husband?" My tongue spoke the words before my mind could stop it.

Linzy shifted her position on the steps and gave me a long look before she replied. "I don't know that Nellie ever had one."

"But what about Schylar and Sylvester?"

Linzy kind of laughed. "Folks around here say that Nellie found them under a cabbage head."

"I know better than that!" I was put out more than a little that Linzy would talk to me as if I were a child. "She had them when her uncle Emery got her in the family way." Nellie hadn't really said for sure that her boys belonged to her Uncle Emery, but it stood to reason since they were the only kids she had to show for that time in her life.

Linzy got to her feet and, with a quick glance at Ednalice to see if she had heard, she took my arm and started walking me toward the gate.

"Who told you such a thing?" she asked, just above a whisper.

"Nellie told me so herself. She said she was telling me about it to warn me. She was afraid the same thing would happen to me."

We had reached the gate, but Linzy made no move to open it. Her eyes studied my face for a long while before she spoke. Then it wasn't what I had expected to hear. I thought she would say that I had misunderstood Nellie or that I was making it all up out of whole cloth.

Instead, Linzy said, "Did Nellie tell you who she suspected might harm you?"

I shook my head. "No. She just said they wouldn't care that they hurt me."

"They?" Linzy said thoughtfully. "Then it's more than one that Nellie has in mind."

I had never told Linzy or anyone else that I thought Schylar and Sylvester had followed me and tried to head me off in the woods. I couldn't swear to it that I had been followed, and I didn't know for sure that they had been lying in wait for me that day, either. They could've just been passing through the woods at the same time that I happened by. But now, I doubted it. Just the way Linzy had said "they," made me think of Schylar and Sylvester and the scare they had given me.

Linzy opened the gate. "You run along home now, Seely," she said. "You'll be safe enough in broad daylight."

I didn't run. It was too hot. But on the other hand, I didn't tarry along the way, either. I think I took my first full breath of air when I crossed the ridge and knew that Mom was in calling distance. I was home safe.

chapter twenty-one

*T*he house had the quiet stillness of an empty house or one where nobody's at home. I thought that Mom was probably taking the shade on the back porch. Our kitchen faced east, and we got the sun and full daylight before places on the other side of the hill even knew that night had ended. And by the same token, we had the first cool shade on the kitchen porch when the sun passed over the ridge of trees. It stood to reason that was where I would find Mom at this time of day.

I went through the front yard, turned the corner of the house, and there on our back porch sat Schylar and Sylvester Fender. I felt as though I had conjured them up with my own mind, just by thinking of them. They had no business at our house. No one had ever told them they were welcome here.

I stopped dead in my tracks, then took a couple of steps back. Schylar and Sylvester smirked and nudged each other. They were staring at me as if they could see right through the cotton dress I had on.

The first thing that came to my mind was that this is what Nellie was trying to warn me about. She had been talking about her own boys, and I hadn't even suspected it. I called for Mom. And even while I was moving away from the house, getting out of their reach, I kept calling for her.

The boys snickered as they got to their feet and started toward me. "Save your breath," one of them said. "Your ma ain't here. She went in the car with Aunt Fanny to Oolitic."

He dragged out the word Oolitic like it was a rope he had tossed to pull me in with and moved slowly across the yard until he was between me and the road.

"We're going to give you a treat that you ain't had before." His amber eyes lit up like a cat's ready to pounce on a mouse. "We almost had you that day on the path, but you gave us the slip among the trees."

At his brother's words, the other one stepped further into the yard, hemming me in till there was no place for me to run. I felt like I had been treed by animals, and now they were sawing the branch off behind me.

I knew there was no way to reason with them, but I thought maybe the threat of what Dad would do to them would hold them. "You'd better stay away from me," I said, as the one from the porch moved in closer to where I stood. "I'll tell my dad on you."

He just sneered at that and kept on coming toward me. "You just tell Johnny Meaders," he said, keeping himself between me and the house. "He ain't going to like what we do to his girl."

The three of us made a slow-moving triangle, with me forming the small, cornered point. Every time I moved, they moved, dancing back and forth, chanting and laughing as the triangle became smaller and smaller.

"I'm not Johnny's girl," I said, thinking that I could distract them by talking. "You're not spiting Johnny Meaders one bit by being here."

They acted as if I hadn't said a word. Their foolish grins didn't change one whit. Only their eyes got bright and glassy as they both rushed me.

"Get away from me!" I screamed and screamed.

Terrified, and anxious to keep them at bay, I turned quickly in a half-circle. There was an opening between me and the house. It was a small chance, but the only one I had left. I whirled to make a dash for the kitchen door, and I saw Nellie Fender step out of the woods and hurry toward me.

"Nellie!" I cried. "Oh, Nellie!" "And I started bawling. Now that I knew I was safe, I couldn't stop crying.

Schylar and Sylvester stopped and began to back away, but Nellie collared them and made them stay.

I found out then that Nellie Fender didn't stutter when she was angry. And she was really mad at her boys. With her arms around me, holding me close and soothing me as if I was the one who belonged to her, she lit into Schylar and Sylvester like a buzz saw. She never once hesitated nor minced her words as she told them what she thought of their behavior.

"It's a good thing for you two," she told them, "that I got here in time to stop what you had in mind."

"We was just fooling," one of them said. "We didn't mean to hurt her. We just aimed to scare her to death."

Their long arms dangled at their sides, and they shuffled their feet as they waited restlessly for Nellie to be finished so they could head for the woods.

Nellie looked at the two red-headed, red-faced boys, meek and quiet, now that they had been caught in their meanness, and told them, "I should've done as Gus Tyson advised me to do and had you both put away years ago. And I'll do it yet," she said quietly, her anger gone. "I'll have you both locked away if you ever lay a hand on Seely or bother her again. And don't you forget it," she added.

One of the boys spoke up belligerently. "Johnny Meaders ought to know we ain't done with him. Not by a long sight."

"Schylar, you forget the Meaderses," Nellie said, stuttering and stumbling over her words again. "Johnny never done you no wrong, and I ain't telling you again to leave him be. You understand me?"

The look she gave the boys was filled with something akin to pity. They nodded sheepishly. "Then get on home, now," she told them.

Schylar and Sylvester yelled back when they reached the road and said something about getting even with

Jack Meaders and making him sorry to be alive. Then they loped off into the woods.

I thought to myself that Schylar and Sylvester had been as scared of their mother's anger as I had been of them. I hadn't noticed the heat while I was trying to stay clear of the Fender boys, but now I found that I was wringing wet with sweat and my mouth was as dry as a cotton sock.

Nellie still had her arm around me as we stepped into the deep shade on the back porch. I moved away to pump a bucketful of fresh water. Then I gave Nellie a cold drink and took a dipper of water for myself.

"Wash your face in that cold water," Nellie told me. "We don't want your ma to catch you looking like you do."

I did as she told me, then sat down with Nellie to cool off on the shady porch.

"I knowed they had something like this in mind," Nellie said. "Ever since the night of the rock fight when your pa came looking for them with a club, I've heard them talk of nothing else but how to get even with him."

"But Dad was just mad because they hit me with a rock."

"I know." Nellie patted my shoulder. "But my boys, they blamed him for taking up with Johnny Meaders against them."

"Why do they hate Johnny so? Johnny told me that, when they were kids, they used to play together."

"It ain't Johnny they hate," Nellie replied. "It's his pa—Jack Meaders." Nellie sighed and shook her head. "I've told them they shouldn't hold a grudge against the man;" she said, her eyes on the spot where the twins had gone into the woods. "That it was the truth he spoke about them. But I guess it was the way he said it that stuck in their craw."

"I don't like the way Jack Meaders says things, either," I told Nellie, "but that's no reason to have hard feelings toward the rest of the family."

"Seely, my boys can't reason, or they never would have come near you." She paused, then went on sadly. "I knowed they wasn't right in the head, not from the day they were born, but I kept hoping that somehow they'd outgrow it. They're grown now," she said, "but their minds still ain't no bigger than when they were babies."

There wasn't a thing I could say to that. I had lumped Schylar and Sylvester together in my mind as one whole piece of meanness for so long that it was hard for me to see them as two separated people, each trying to make do with less than their share of common sense. And even then, it wasn't until I heard the tenderness in Nellie's voice as she spoke of them that I realized that, even with their simple-mindedness and all the trouble they had caused her, Schylar and Sylvester were just as dear to Nellie Fender as Robert was to Mom.

I knew this just as surely as if she had told me so. But I couldn't understand how it could be true. Couldn't Nellie see for herself that Schylar and Sylvester were a walking bag of trouble, I thought to myself. They're like a gunny sack full of spite and meanness just waiting the chance to spill out and cover us all with pain and misery. And then, I thought, Nellie would be the one who was hurt the worst when that happened.

Nellie sat on the porch and talked to me until Aunt Fanny's car came roaring over the ridge, bringing a cloud of dust and Mom home with it. Then she stood up and said she'd best get back to her side of the hill.

"Folks will be mighty curious about me frittering away my time on your back porch," Nellie said, smiling at me.

I smiled, too. Then laughed out loud as I told her, "Linzy Meaders said once that you wasn't one to waste a day just a-sittin' and a-rockin', but if you had a mind to do it, she told me that you wouldn't care two hoots what folks thought about it."

Nellie laughed, then settled back in her chair to wait for Fanny Phillips to stop at our house.

Fanny didn't linger. She had a drink of water, offered Nellie a lift home in the car, and they both left soon afterwards.

"It's funny how Nellie Fender has taken such a liking to you," Mom said, as she watched the car go out of sight over the ridge. "But then," she added, "I suppose with those two backward boys of hers, she gets a yearning to talk to a sensible girl once in a while."

I appreciated Mom thinking that I was a sensible girl, but not to the point where I would tell her the real reason why Nellie was here with me. I let on to her that she was right in supposing that Nellie had walked home with me as usual, then stayed to visit a spell. It would never do for Mom to know what had really taken place here today. If she found out about it, she would never let me out of her sight again as long as I lived. And she would harp on it from now until doomsday.

chapter twenty-two

I never breathed a word to a soul about finding the Fender boys waiting for me that day when I got home. And no one ever mentioned their names to me. But I felt like everyone knew somehow about what Schylar and Sylvester had tried to do.

It seemed like all of a sudden Mom and Robert took to walking to the Meaders' with me each day. Or else Linzy found a good reason to come to our house early in the morning, and I went home with her. Nellie still met me at the edge of the trees and kept me company through the woods. But she never spoke of Schylar and Sylvester, nor mentioned that day they had cornered me in our back yard. It was as though nothing out of the ordinary had ever happened.

I guess the work slacked off at Gus Tyson's lumber

yard about that time. Johnny and Byron didn't seem so busy now, and I saw them more often. Every afternoon when the whistle blew for quitting time at the mill, I could almost count the minutes until they would be sprawled on the steps to our back porch. They even gave up swimming in the blue hole after work just to hang around our house until dark.

It was during this time that the plant at Crowe closed down for a week, and Dad was home every day. I thought at first he would get tired of seeing the boys every night for supper and send them packing. But he didn't say anything to them about it. He seemed to find it amusing.

One afternoon when we heard the quitting whistle blow at the mill, Dad glanced at the clock, grinned at Mom, and said, "Well, in a few minutes, Miles Standish and John Alden will be here again for supper."

I knew Longfellow's story of Priscilla, but I didn't catch Dad's meaning. Not until later that evening when I was sitting spraddled-legged on the steps to get my breath after a fast game of tag ball with the boys. Then he made it clear to me.

Dad and Mom had brought kitchen chairs to the porch so they could sit and watch us kids play ball. When it got so dark they couldn't see us, Dad called the game. Soon afterwards, Johnny and Byron went home.

Dad looked at me and laughed. "Seely, it's a wonder to me how you ever got one beau," he said, "let alone two boyfriends coming by here every night to see you."

I sat up straight against the porch post and smoothed

my skirt over my knees. "They're not boyfriends," I said. "Not the beau kind, anyhow."

"Now, Seely." He laughed, teasing me.

"They're not boyfriends," I repeated. Then for his benefit, I explained. "There are no girls around here to be friends with, so I had to make friends of the boys."

I got up to go to my room. "It's not the same thing as having a beau," I told Dad, and closed the screen door quietly behind me.

Dad never mentioned anything more about my friendship with Johnny and Byron. I caught quick glances between him and Mom when they thought I wasn't watching, but that was all. On Saturday, when we went to Oolitic, Dad didn't bat an eye when he saw Johnny and Byron waiting in front of the Rainbow Store. Not even when Mom said, "Seely, run along and have your soda with the boys. I'll keep Robert with me."

As I climbed out of the car, Mom said, "Mind you, be back here in an hour."

She always cautioned me about the time. And we never had more than an hour. But it was the best sixty minutes of the whole week.

I don't know why Nellie Fender went to prayer meeting with us the next Sunday. Maybe she thought if she was along, Schylar and Sylvester would behave themselves and leave us alone on the way there and back. Or she might have got tired of Mom and Linzy asking her to go and wanted to hush them up. But whatever she had in mind, when we got to the Fender house that evening, Nellie had on her best dress and was waiting for us at the gate.

We got to the schoolhouse at the same time as the Reverend Mister Paully. He spoke to Mom and Linzy, calling them by name, then smiled a slow smile and took Nellie Fender by the hand.

"Praise the Lord," he said. "I've waited a long time to see you enter the house of God."

The preacher spoke softly. Nellie just smiled and ducked her head, then followed Mom and Linzy to their seats. I waited around outside for a while, hoping to catch a glimpse of Johnny and Byron among the other boys. But when I didn't see them, I went on inside and sat down.

This turned out to be one of the preacher's more quiet sermons. The kind that I liked. He spoke of the one sheep that had strayed from the fold and was feared lost forever but was now found. Then he went on to tell of the feast and rejoicing when the wayward son returned to his home.

" 'We rejoice and praise God,' the father said. 'I thought he was lost, but now he has been found.' " The Reverend Mister Paully finished his sermon speaking softly. His eyes never left Nellie Fender's face. But I don't believe Nellie even noticed. She had kept her head down during most of his sermon.

I liked Mister Paully when he preached quietly. Everyone in the room just sat back and rested while they listened to him, and a look of peace settled over their faces.

When we started to leave, Linzy said the preacher was tired. He wasn't up to rousing the people and making them see the light of repentance tonight. But I thought it was just as well that he didn't get them all stirred up and agitated. They had come to prayer meeting looking weary and speaking sharply to their kids. And now they were smiling as they called the children to them and bid one another a cheerful good-night.

Nellie didn't have much to say on the short walk to her house, but I guess she liked going to the meeting. When she turned toward her gate, she said, "I'll see you all next Sunday," just as though she had been going to prayer meeting with us right along.

Mom and Linzy waited until a light came on in Nellie's house, then we went on, the two of them talking quietly. I was trying to corral Robert and Ednalice and keep them out of the side ditches.

The night was pitch black, and the little crest of new moon didn't help a bit when it came to seeing the ruts and chuckholes in the road. We almost walked right by the lane leading to the Meaders' house before we saw it. Linzy took Ednalice off my hands, said she would see me tomorrow, and soon faded into the dark woods on their way home.

I still went over to the Meaders' house every day, even though Grandma Stoner had improved steadily and, by this time, there was nothing the matter with her but old age and crankiness. Linzy said she wanted me there to help her, and I liked the money she gave me every Saturday, so I went.

"The old truck's gone!" Mom spoke with a note of surprise. "I wonder when Hallam Henderson came and hauled it away."

I said that I had grown so used to seeing it, I couldn't remember now whether it had been there yesterday or not.

"I'll ask Rob," she said. "He'll know."

But Dad was just as puzzled as we were about the truck being moved. He said that Hallam hadn't mentioned it to him.

"It gave me quite a turn," Mom said. "As long as that old rattletrap sat there, I felt like a visitor to these parts. But now that the truck has been taken away, we may never get out of here."

I thought she was going to start complaining to Dad again because we hadn't made it out of the hills, and I didn't want to hear it. I picked up a lamp, told Robert to come with me, and we went to bed.

chapter twenty-three

*I*t was daylight the next morning, but the sun wasn't up yet. I shouldn't have been. But the sounds from the kitchen as Mom fixed Dad's breakfast had wakened me, and the smell of bacon frying had lured me out to the table.

"It's funny that Hallam Henderson didn't come here to the house and tell you he was taking it." Mom was still worrying about the disappearance of the truck. "He knew you were at home," she added.

Dad said that Mom should forget that damn truck, that he would speak to Hallam about it today. "But as busy as we've been after shut-down," he added, "don't expect me home until you see me coming."

Shortly after that, Dad got in the blue Buick and left for work.

His place at the table hadn't had time to cool, when Linzy Meaders opened the door and stepped into the kitchen. She was dragging Ednalice by one hand and trying to hold her cotton wrapper together with the other. They were both barefoot, bedraggled, and in their night clothes.

Mom took one look at Linzy's sooty, tear-streaked face, then pulled Dad's chair back from the table and gently eased her into it. "Now, tell me what's gone wrong," Mom said softly.

"It must've been a spark from the chimney that started it," Linzy wearily pushed the tangled hair from her face. "I can't see it no other way," she said.

"Oh, my God! You've had a fire!" Mom put her hand to her mouth, then bent over Linzy to comfort her.

Mom was terrified of us having a house fire. She went through each day checking the stove pipe to see if it was red hot and watching the flue for sparks. She worried constantly that the house would catch fire and burn down around us. I've no doubt in my mind that even while she slept, Mom unconsciously sniffed for the smell of smoke.

Linzy nodded her head, then folded her arms on the table and hid her face in them. Mom touched Linzy's shoulder. "Are you all right?" she asked gently. Then, "How did it happen?"

"I don't know," Linzy said, moving her head back and forth on her arms. "I just don't know."

A moment passed, then Linzy raised her head and

wiped at her face with a corner of her robe. Mom handed her a wet cloth, but Linzy just held it in her hand and continued to shake her head, as if she still couldn't believe it had happened.

"Jack had to be in Birdseye today for early deliveries," Linzy said, as if starting at the very beginning she would be able to get it all straight in her mind. "I built a fire and made him a bite to eat, but I let the fire die. Then when he left about four o'clock, I went back to bed. The barking of the dog roused me," she went on. "I don't know how long I listened to that animal bark and growl before I was fully aroused, but when I woke, the room was full of smoke and the kitchen a blaze of fire."

Linzy paused and reached for the cup of coffee that Mom had placed in front of her. "I got Ednalice out of the house with no trouble at all," she said. "But when I went back for Grandma Stoner, she wasn't in her bed, and I couldn't find her."

Mom said, "Don't go blaming yourself, now. You did all you could do for her."

"But she would've burned with the house if it hadn't been for Johnny and Byron," Linzy said.

She took a deep breath and sat up straighter in Dad's chair. "I guess I owe thanks to Schylar and Sylvester Fender for being on the road to the sawmill this morning," she said. "Otherwise, Johnny and Byron wouldn't have taken the path by our house to work today. They were keeping out of the Fender boys' way when they saw the smoke and came running to the burning house."

Her voice broke, and she had to breathe deeply before she could go on. "They carried her out," Linzy said. "But by that time, she'd breathed too much smoke. Grandma was dead."

Everything was quiet. No one said anything for a long while. Then Mom said, "Your grandma lived a good long life."

That didn't seem like much to say about one who had died, I thought. Somehow, not enough to pass on to the ones who were left to grieve their passing. But it seemed to satisfy Linzy. Even to please her, in a way.

She looked up at Mom, and I saw the trace of a smile cross her face. "Kate Stoner wasn't really blood kin," Linzy said. "But she treated me kinder than any kin would have." She sighed and turned her face to the table. "I don't know what we would've done five years ago if she hadn't taken pity and helped us."

Mom waited for Linzy to go on, and when she didn't, Mom said, "Those were hard times back then. Everyone needed help, and there was none to come by. I'd say that you were right fortunate to have someone you could count on."

"I could always count on Grandma Stoner," Linzy replied.

The silence stretched on while Mom and Linzy sipped at their coffee. Finally Linzy said, "We were living in Kentucky, then. Pineville, Kentucky."

She made a small bitter sound that could've passed for a laugh. "Jack couldn't get work, and the young'uns were hungry. When Kate Stoner heard of our hard times, she sent word that we were to come and live with her. She'd feed the kids, she said. Now she's dead," Linzy finished sadly, "and I can't even hold a wake for her."

"You'll stay here with us," Mom told Linzy. "We have three empty rooms, and Grandma can be laid out in that room at the foot of the stairs. We've never used it," she added. As if it could matter to Grandma Stoner whether it was a used room, or not.

Linzy said they couldn't impose on us. They would be too much trouble. "And besides that," she added, "the house ain't been built yet that will hold two families peaceably."

But Mom said she'd not hear another word. "When I came as a stranger to these parts, you offered room and board to me and the young'uns. And now that we're friends and neighbors, you can't rightly refuse when I offer the same to you."

It was settled. Jack and Linzy Meaders would live in our three empty rooms with Ednalice, and Johnny could move in with Byron Tyson and stay at Aunt Fanny's house in Jubilee. It pleased Mom. But I thought that Dad was liable to raise hell and put a choke under it when he got home and found Jack Meaders was living under the same roof with him.

Just last week, Dad had remarked that the less he saw of Jack Meaders, the better he liked it. He said he wouldn't trust the man any farther than he could throw the Meaders' mule. Mom had replied that she didn't favor his company either, but Linzy was another matter. "She's got her work cut out for her." Mom had sighed. "Putting up with that man and his notions can't be easy."

Now it looked as if we would all get a taste of the rough time that Linzy had been getting in full ration for years.

Mom brought some old clothes that I had outgrown for Ednalice to put on and took Linzy to her bedroom, saying she was to help herself to anything she needed from Mom's own meager wardrobe. Then while Linzy and Ednalice were getting washed and dressed, Mom put a pan of biscuits in the oven and cooked a big kettle of rolled oats for our breakfast.

I woke Robert and told him to hurry and get dressed. Breakfast was ready. "Ednalice will be living here with us for a while," I said. "So you behave yourself and be nice to her."

Robert looked at me with wide-eyed innocence, as if he had been caught doing something he knew he shouldn't. "I'm nice to her," he said. "Ednalice pushes me in the swing and lets be the first to ride the tricycle every time."

I said, "Robert, you've got it backwards. That's when Ednalice is being nice to you." And took him in to breakfast.

After we had finished eating, Mom told me to take the kids for a walk. "Just to get them out of the house for a spell," she said.

When I asked about the dirty dishes, Mom gave me a long look. "Never mind the dishes," she said. "Do as I tell you."

The sun felt warm to my back as we left the house and walked up the dirt road. But as soon as we had crossed the spine of the hill and started down the other side, we lost the warmth of the sun in the deep shade of the trees, and it turned chilly. Robert and Ednalice complained of the coolness and ran from one patch of sunshine to another trying to get warm. But I just poked along. I knew the coolness wouldn't last long. As soon as the day got a little older, it would be sweltering hot and impossible to find a cool place.

When we got to the pike, Robert turned up the hill. He said he wanted to show Ednalice where we had camped for two days.

"The old truck's gone," he told her. "Hallam Henderson came and got it. But I can find the place anyhow," he assured her.

About halfway up the hill we saw fresh tire tracks leading into the woods and heading straight for the steepest, deepest gully this side of the White River cuts. We followed the mashed-down weeds and broken brush through the woods to the rim of the ravine, and there far below us was the bent and battered junk of the old truck that had brought us to this place.

Robert's face was a picture of indignation and dismay. "Hallam didn't take it," he said. "Someone's wrecked it."

It had taken more than one, I thought, with all muscles and no brains, to push that truck down the hill and off the road. And especially for the final shove that had sent the truck rolling to the bottom of the ravine.

"Dad told Mom the day we got here that that truck wasn't going another mile," Robert said solemnly.

Ednalice looked at the jumbled mess of bent metal, then turned to face Robert. "It's a cinch it won't move again now," she replied just as solemnly.

And more than likely, I thought, neither will we.

We were a quiet, sober trio as we went on to our old camping place. But once we were there, Robert became his usual talkative self. He ran up the slope, laughing and chattering like a blue jay, and stopped near the pile of smoke-blackened stones that had been our cook fire.

"This was the stove," he told Ednalice, when she stood beside him. "Mom cooked here. We ate there." His hand pointed to one side of the fireplace. "And we slept under the trees."

He took her hand and led her to where each piece of furniture had been. "That was when we didn't have a house to put things in," Robert said.

"We don't have a house, now," Ednalice said. "And if we did, we wouldn't have a stick of anything to put in it."

Robert smiled, and his face took on a protective look as he moved closer to her. "That's all right," he said. "I do, and you can live in my house with me forever and ever."

That was the only time I heard the kids refer to the house fire in any way. And Ednalice never once mentioned Grandma Stoner. I wondered if she even realized what had happened. She didn't act like it.

Robert and Ednalice ran ahead of me into the woods,

going in the general direction of the path I had used every day this summer to get to the Meaders' place. I followed them. I thought that we could take the path when we came to it and get back to the dirt lane from there. But somehow, we missed the path and came out on the far side of the woods, wading into a meadow that was knee deep in tickle grass, foxtail, and wild flowers.

"Oh, look!" Robert cried. "A whole field full of flowers."

He opened his arms as if the spread from fingertip to fingertip would take in the wide, sunny meadow.

"We can pick these flowers," Ednalice told Robert. "They don't belong to anyone."

She broke a stem of orange and black-speckled tiger lily, then moved on to a clump of creamy Queen Anne's lace and began to break off the flowers. Robert looked askance at her actions, but when I didn't say no, he started picking the blue ragged robins and white daisies that grew thick around his feet.

"Gather all you want," I said. "Mom and Linzy can use them for Grandma Stoner's wake." But the kids weren't listening to me. Their heads were filled with the sunshine and wild flowers and visions of taking every bright blossom they could lay their hands on.

They ran in every direction, breaking long stems, and gathering flowers by the handful. When their fingers wouldn't meet around a bunch, they laid the flowers across their arms like stacking stove wood to carry inside.

The kids would soon have their arms filled with

flowers and they would want to go straight home from here so the flowers wouldn't wilt in the hot sun. I looked at the field and the trees on all four sides of us, trying to determine the shortest and quickest way to get to the house. It was then I realized that nothing was familiar to me. I didn't know the way home. I was lost.

The kids were depending on me to keep them safe and sound. I was older and supposed to know something about directions. Yet I had allowed myself to get lost and had taken them with me. Why hadn't I paid attention to where we were going?

When I had stopped berating myself for being so stupid, I looked at the sun. That should tell me something. In the early morning it rose facing our kitchen window, then it traveled in a direct route over our house toward the ridge of trees and the pike road beyond.

Now the sun was tilted about two hours to the west of us, almost directly above the ridge. I figured if I kept the sun to my right and angled off across the narrow end of the meadow, we should come out of the woods in front of our house.

While I still had my bearings, I wanted to get started, so I called the kids to me. "Come on. We're going home, now," I told them.

They stopped to pick a few more tiger lilies along the way, then followed me without question toward the far side of the meadow and the deep woods beyond.

I didn't miss my bearings by very much. We went through a good-sized stand of black oak and sugar gum trees. Then we came out in the clearing across from our house, the place where I had seen Nellie Fender step from the woods the day her boys had me cornered in our back yard.

Robert and Ednalice started running toward the house as soon as it came in sight. But after a few steps, we all stopped and just stared. There was so much furniture and stuff piled on the back porch that we couldn't see the door. It looked like the second-hand junk store in Oolitic had moved to Gus Tyson's house.

Fanny Phillip's car sat in front of the house, and when we got inside, I saw that she hadn't come alone. Nellie Fender was there, also. They were helping Linzy to get settled in the other half of our house.

"Where did all these things come from?" I asked.

They had already set up a daybed in the room at the foot of the stairs, and there were a half-dozen chairs lined up along one wall.

Nellie Fender looked up and smiled. Mom said, "It's about time you were getting here." But it was Aunt Fanny who answered my question.

"As soon as the neighbors heard about the fire, they carried in everything they could spare to help Linzy set up housekeeping again," she said.

Linzy arranged the field flowers in a fruit jar, and Nellie brought a stand table from the back porch to set it on. "These will look right pretty in here," Linzy said, "when they bring Grandma home."

Mom and Aunt Fanny agreed that the wild flowers made a real pretty bouquet and went on hanging curtains at the three windows. The curtains didn't match, but it looked better than the bare window glass staring you in the face.

In the hustle and bustle of getting the house ready for Grandma's wake, I completely forgot to tell Mom that we had found the old truck torn to pieces at the bottom of a ravine. And if Robert and Ednalice ever thought of it, they didn't mention it.

I watched for a while, then Mom said that I should make myself useful. "Carry those boxes upstairs," she said, pointing to a stack of cardboard cartons. "And when you're done, sort the clothing and put it away."

Robert and Ednalice helped me lug the boxes upstairs, then tore into them like it was Christmas morning. Looking and hoping, I suppose, to find something special inside. But they soon gave it up and stepped back from the empty cartons with a puzzled and disappointed look on their faces.

I was disappointed, too. Here it was past the middle of summer, and I would've bet anyone that most of the time it was a hundred and ten in the shade, but one would have thought it was below zero of a freezing December from the clothes that the neighbors had sent for Linzy to use.

I counted six coats and just as many heavy sweaters, before I finally stopped counting and just stuffed them back in the box. I put to one side the few things they could wear now. And most of that was aprons, men's shirts, and cotton house dresses that were three sizes too big for Linzy.

* * *

The house was all cleaned and ready for her when they brought Grandma Stoner home the next day. They put her in the room at the foot of the stairs, just as Mom said they could, and afterwards everyone walked on tiptoe from room to room, and no one ever spoke above a whisper.

chapter twenty-four

*A*ll that afternoon, the neighbor women trooped in to pay their respects to the old woman. They came to the kitchen to drink Mom's coffee, then stood about the room in little bunches to hash over the latest gossip. One woman brought a big three-layer cake, and after that I was kept busy washing cups and saucers and cake plates so there would be enough dishes to go around.

Near evening time, after he had finished his day's work, the Reverend Mister Paully came to call. He and Linzy sat alone in the front room and talked quietly for a long time. Once I heard his voice raised in prayer. But even then, I couldn't hear what he was saying. I guess it must have been some comfort to Linzy to have the preacher there. She seemed more at ease and, as Mom said, more able to go on when he had gone.

By nightfall, there was just Nellie Fender and Fanny Phillips left at the house to sit up with Mom and Linzy at Grandma Stoner's wake. They said they would have to take turns sitting up with her. While one catnapped on the daybed, the others would keep watch. "We don't dare to leave the body untended," Linzy said, with a meaningful look at the other three women.

I wondered what she thought Grandma could do now. She certainly wasn't going anywhere under her own power. And I doubted that anyone would try to steal her. Linzy's words puzzled me. I decided I would stay awake tonight also. And I would find out for myself why Grandma had to be watched, even after she was dead.

Mom sent us kids to bed early, and since Linzy wouldn't be upstairs with her, Ednalice was allowed to sleep with Robert in his bed. They whispered and giggled for a while, then I heard their deep, even breathing and I knew they had gone to sleep.

I forced myself to stay awake. I wanted to listen to whatever went on in the other room. I turned on my stomach and folded my arms on the scrunched-up pillow to prop my head. Then I could hear every word just as plain as if I had been in the same room with them.

I heard Mom say it was stuffy in there. And then the scrape of a window being raised.

"Zel, don't open it too wide." That was Aunt Fanny's voice. "I've heard tell that a pack of cats can smell a corpse for a mile away and do about anything to get to it."

"I've heard that!" Nellie stammered.

The window frame screaked as Mom lowered the window.

"When we were sitting up with old Uncle John Knight," Linzy said, "cats yowled and scratched at the doors until finally a couple of the boys had to take a fiery stick and drive them away."

"Now that's a caution," Mom said. "I've heard of dogs howling around the house when a member of the family dies, but never had any dealings with cats."

"We won't hear no howling from that fool hound of ours," Linzy said. "When the heat from the fire popped the window lights, the dog crawled back under the house and died in the fire."

Everything was quiet in the room for a moment, then I heard Aunt Fanny say, "Funny things happen when a body's soul leaves this world." She cleared her throat, and I cocked my head to one side so I could hear better.

"I recollect my mother telling about the night they held the wake for my grandfather Dunley. From what she said then, I figure that Grandfather must have been laid out in a room pretty much the same as this one." Aunt Fanny paused, and I could imagine that she was eyeing the room from one end to the other. Then she went on. "It had a wide staircase going up one wall behind the coffin, and Mother said they had set a coal-oil lamp on the newel-post to light his face and give the folks a decent viewing. Then right on the stroke of midnight, that oil lamp fell from its place on the stair railing and rolled straight as a die to the old man's coffin. It flared up once, bright enough to blind a body, then went out, leaving the room in total darkness."

"Well, I'll swear, I never heard of such a thing," Linzy said. "It's a wonder on earth that the lamp didn't explode and kill them all."

"There's an unseen hand that controls these things," Aunt Fanny said ominously.

Mom didn't say anything, but I could hear the rocking chair going like sixty as she digested Aunt Fanny's story.

But Aunt Fanny wasn't finished with her tale yet. She took a deep breath and said, "My mother swore that later on that night a huge ball of orange fire appeared outside the bedroom window and hovered there for a moment. Then it moved to the meadow, bounced down to the lower pasture, and faded into the night, taking Grandfather's mortal soul with it."

Aunt Fanny gave a great sigh of satisfaction at a story well told, and I knew just as well as if I could see them that Mom, Linzy, and Nellie Fender were looking over their shoulders toward the unshaded windows and probably wishing for daylight.

I shivered in my warm bed and pulled the sheet up to cover my face. Even if I smothered to death, I wasn't listening to any more of their talk. Let them scare themselves with their unbelievable tales, I thought, but they weren't frightening me.

I slept then. But my dreams were filled with yowling cats, howling dogs, and great balls of fire that ballooned in my room and hovered over my bed, just waiting for my mortal soul.

I awoke to broad daylight and a silence so complete that I thought I must be the only one left on the place. I looked at Robert's empty bed and told myself that having Ednalice here was a godsend. Robert had gotten out of bed this morning without any help from me.

I dressed, brushed my hair, and hurried to the kitchen. The door to the room where they had put Grandma Stoner was closed, but just the same, after the stories I had heard the night before, I didn't want to be alone in the house with her.

I was dishing up oatmeal from a kettle on the back of the stove when Mom came in from outside. "We've all had our breakfast, and Aunt Fanny and Nellie have gone home to get ready for the funeral." She gave me and my heaped-up bowl a disapproving look. "The undertaker will be here any minute to carry Grandma Stoner to the church, and you'll still be eating oatmeal."

"That's all right," I said and took a deep breath. "I'm not going, anyway."

"The funeral's at ten," Mom said. "And you be ready when Fanny gets here to carry us to town."

Linzy came in then. She had on Mom's one good Sunday dress. Mom was wearing an old one. But she had washed and ironed it, and the dress looked good enough to wear any place. Even to a funeral.

"I probably should have made some attempt to get a-hold of Jack and tell him about the fire," Linzy said. "But I figure he might as well finish the week's work before he comes home." She thought for a moment, then smiled at Mom. "There's nothing he could do about it, anyhow. Not now," she added. "And Grandma would've understood why I didn't want him here till after she was buried."

Mom said that she thought Linzy had done the right thing. No one could fault her for the way she had handled it. "Had he been here," Mom added, "you'd have had it all to do, anyway."

Fanny Phillips came to take Mom and Linzy to the funeral just as I was taking my last bite of rolled oats, and the hearse for Grandma rolled up close behind her.

"I knew it," Mom said. "Fanny's here, and you're still eating."

Mom stepped to the door and called for Aunt Fanny to come on in. "The kids are not ready yet," she said.

"I don't like taking Ednalice to the funeral," Linzy said. "But there's no way around it. She can't stay here alone."

I looked at Mom before I spoke, hoping against all reason that she would see the logic in my words and agree with me.

"I'll stay here and look after Ednalice and Robert," I told Linzy. "I don't like funerals."

Linzy looked first at Mom, then back to me. Mom didn't say anything, so I explained. "I've been to one already," I said, "and that one will last me a whole lifetime."

I could feel Mom's eyes on my face, but I wouldn't look her way. Finally she said, "I don't know why I didn't think of that." Then real softly she added, "A funeral's no place for a couple of young'uns."

When the dust had settled behind the hearse and the car, which followed close behind it, I called Robert and Ednalice to me. "Let's walk to the pike road and meet the mailman," I said. "Maybe we'll get a letter from Julie."

Mom said that almost every day. But we'd had only one letter from Julie since we had got here. And that one said not to expect her home when school was out. She had a job she liked, she wrote, and besides that, it didn't sound like there was anything for her in Jubilee.

Dad had read the letter, and then said, "Julie's right. We can't expect her to give up a good job just to come down here and twiddle her thumbs."

But Mom felt differently about it. "If she thought anything of her family, Julie would want to come home."

"Damn it, Zel," Dad shouted. "That's got nothing to do with it." Then, "Where would you be now if you hadn't left your family?" he asked.

Mom had opened her mouth to tell him, but I guess she had thought it best not to say. She shut her mouth, turned away, and carried the letter with her when she left the room. We hadn't heard a word from Julie since then.

Robert asked now why I thought we might get a letter today. "We never get any mail," he told Ednalice.

"This would be a good day for Julie to write," I said, and believed every word I spoke.

A letter from Julie would ease Mom's mind and give her something to think on besides death, fires, and funerals, I thought. And it might even put Dad in a better frame of mind and make him more acceptable to the notion of having Jack Meaders in the house.

The mailman waved at us and drove right on by our mailbox. Robert said, "See that? I told you we didn't get letters."

He wasn't crowing about being right, yet he didn't seem disappointed, either. He was just pointing out an obvious fact to Ednalice. Robert didn't miss Julie the way I did, I thought, and realized then that I didn't miss her as much as I had at the first.

On the way back to the house, we saw Schylar and Sylvester Fender skulking through the woods, but they didn't see us. I wasn't afraid of them when I had Robert and Ednalice with me. They wouldn't dare to come near while the kids were along. But I shushed Robert's chatter anyway and walked on tiptoe until the Fender boys had disappeared from sight among the trees.

I wondered why Schylar and Sylvester always appeared to be sneaking. Even when they were out in the open, they had a secretive look about them. I guess it was the way they had of walking. They didn't step along the way we did, but walked with their heads cocked to one side and slightly bent forward, as if listening and looking for something out of place.

It wasn't quite noon yet, when Fanny Phillips

brought Mom and Linzy Meaders home from the funeral, but she didn't come in the house. As soon as Mom and Linzy stepped foot on the ground, Fanny turned the car around, waved, and went directly back down the road toward town.

Mom watched as the car topped the rise and faded from sight behind the ridge, then she followed Linzy into the house.

"I'm glad that's over," she said, slipping a bib apron over her head and tying the strings. "Now we can start praying for rain to settle the dust and cool things down a bit."

Linzy released a great sigh, as if she had been holding her breath for three days. "Had it rained earlier," she said, "we'd have had to haul Grandma to the church by mule and wagon. The hearse would never have made it down that dirt road.

That was for sure, I thought. Whenever we'd had a hard rain this summer, Dad had had to leave the car at the end of the lane and walk back to the house. "I know your garden needs the moisture," he told Mom one afternoon while he was cleaning the mud from his shoes. "But does it have to rain every damn Friday and Saturday!"

Mom replied that it didn't rain every week. It just seemed that way to him because he had to wade mud once in a while to get home. "Having that automobile has spoiled you for walking," she had added.

I guess Mom's mind had been running in the same channel as mine. She said now, "Much as we need it, it wouldn't hurt to hold off asking for rain till after the men get home."

"And leave again," Linzy laughed. "We'd better pray that Jack and Rob don't draw and quarter us for throwing them together under the same roof."

"I've thought of that, too," Mom said soberly.

Although they made light of it, I could tell that Mom and Linzy felt more than a little anxious about the coming weekend. Dad and Jack Meaders would be coming home at the same time on Saturday, and there would be no chance to prepare either of them for the other's presence in the house. All we could do, I thought, was to cross our fingers and hope for the best.

chapter twenty-five

Mom and Linzy shifted the furniture from one room to another, setting the house in order and balancing their belongings to make sure that both families had what they needed to live comfortably. Mom laughed and said that she and Linzy worked together like a well-matched team of horses. Linzy said she felt like a workhorse. And we all laughed.

Then Linzy got serious. "We probably should've stayed in Kentucky near kinfolk," she said. "And never come up north in the first place."

Mom smiled fondly on her and replied, "Then I would never have gotten to know you, Linzy. And that would've been a shame."

I liked listening to Mom and Linzy talk as they went

about their chores. Unless Mom told me in no uncertain terms to stay with Robert and Ednalice, I left the kids to their own schemes and followed her and Linzy from room to room. I helped when they needed me, but mostly I just listened. I didn't learn much. I think they kept a pretty tight rein on their tongues while I was in the room.

Once, Mom said, "Seely, can't you find something to do elsewhere?" And as soon as I was out the door, I heard her tell Linzy, "A year ago I couldn't find that girl from daylight to dark. Now, I can't turn around that she's not underfoot, listening to every word I say."

Linzy laughed. "Pay her no mind, Zel. Seely's at that curious age when a girl wants to know everything it has taken her mother forty years to find out about."

While Mom and Linzy were getting supper ready I went to my room and got out my notebook. This was a brand new one with nothing but my name written on the first page. I had used up all the clean pages in my old notebook, so the first time that Linzy ever gave me money for helping with Grandma Stoner, I had spent every penny of it on paper and pencils. Then the next time I got paid, I bought a small wooden chest from the junk store in Oolitic. Mom said it was a jewelry box. But I kept my paper, notebooks, and pencils in it.

I didn't have anything special today that I wanted to put on paper to keep. I would've liked to write down and save the warm happy feeling that had filled the house since Linzy and Ednalice had come to live with us. But I didn't know how to express this in words.

I sat with my notebook open on my lap and hoped with all my heart that Dad and Jack Meaders wouldn't act up when they got home. It would upset Mom and Linzy and take all their pleasure out of being together in this house. It wouldn't solve anything, I thought, or do anyone a bit of good.

Dad and Jack Meaders came home on Saturday within a few minutes of each other. Jack got there first. We were just finishing our noon meal when he stepped into the kitchen, carrying his suit coat over his shoulder and wiping sweat from his face with a bare hand.

"Whoo-e-e-e," he said, flinging drops of moisture away with a snap of his fingers. "It's hotter than a bitch wolf out there today."

Mom flushed red to the roots of her auburn hair, and her brown eyes snapped with sudden anger. "Seely, take the young'uns to play in the shade," she said in a deceptively soft voice. "And you stay there with them," she added.

Jack Meaders is in for it now, I thought, as I let the screen door swing shut behind me. Linzy might not stand up to her husband, but Mom would have no compunctions about speaking her mind to him. She didn't like him anyhow.

I took a couple of steps, then stopped to listen.

"We've got to have an understanding about that kind of language. . . ." I heard Mom say. Then the wooden door closed with a soft click, cutting off the rest of her words.

As I hurried to catch up with Robert and Ednalice, I thought that Mom would rather roast in that hot kitchen then take a chance on me hearing what she had to say to Jack Meaders.

Whatever it was, it didn't take her long to get it said. When Robert, Ednalice, and I followed Dad into the house a little later, the kitchen door stood wide open. Mom was standing quietly at one side of the table, while Linzy watched Jack on the other side.

Dad stopped short just inside the door, his eyes going first to Mom's flushed face, then to the figure of Jack Meaders.

"Zel, what the hell is going on here?"

"That's what I'd like to know!" Jack Meaders bellowed before Mom had a chance to open her mouth. "I got the word that I was to come straight here," Jack went on. "Yet I'd no more than stepped foot into this house when your woman lit into me. Giving orders, by damn, as if I lived here!"

"Jack, we do live here," Linzy said quietly. "I've been trying to tell you, but you wouldn't listen."

Jack said, "Wouldn't listen . . ."

Then Dad broke in. "I'd like to know . . ."

I guess they both realized at the same time what Linzy had said. They turned toward Mom, but Dad beat Jack Meaders to the punch this time and got his say in first.

"Zel, suppose you tell me what this is all about."

Mom went to stand beside Linzy Meaders and put her arm lightly around Linzy's waist. "Rob, you and Jack sit down," she said. "We'll put your dinner on the table and we can talk while you eat."

Without another word, Mom and Linzy went to the stove and began to fill two plates for the men.

Dad motioned Jack toward the table. "We might as well do as she says," Dad said. "We'll not find out a damn thing till they're ready to tell us."

He pulled out a chair for Jack Meaders, then moved to his place at the end of the table and sat down. Mom and Linzy set the heaped plates in front of the men, then Mom poured coffee before she sat down.

Mom told them then how Grandma Stoner's house had burned to the ground and Grandma had died in the fire. Linzy had come to our house for help, Mom said. "With not a stitch left in the world but the clothes on her back." She got up and went to the stove for more food.

"We had these three big rooms just going to waste," Mom went on, "and Linzy needed a place to live. It was as simple as that."

Dad held up a hand to stop her words. "You didn't say how you women figured to furnish them rooms. A man can't sleep on the floor, and we've no extra beds to spare."

"There was hardly time to ponder that problem," Mom replied. "Word of the fire spread like the wind through the hills and hollows. Folks brought in beds, dressers, and tables and chairs and piled them on our back porch for Linzy to use."

She picked up the coffeepot and moved around the table filling their cups. "We've been all week making them rooms fit to live in," Mom added. "It would be a shame for the work to go for nothing."

"For God's sake, Zel, stop flitting about and light somewhere," Jack Meaders said. "There's no need to make over us like we're company. We live here." Then he laughed like a braying jackass.

Dad frowned as he leaned back in his chair, took out his pipe, and began to fill it from a pouch in his shirt pocket. He tamped the tobacco down and lit it, taking deep drags on the pipe and blowing great puffs of smoke while he waited for Jack Meaders to stop laughing.

"Now that's yet to be decided," Dad said calmly, when Jack had quieted down. "You live here, you'll buy your own groceries and pay for your rooms."

Mom said, "Rob!" in astonishment.

Jack Meaders nodded his head. "Wouldn't have it any other way."

"Then I guess it's settled," Dad said, his face hidden behind a cloud of smoke. "You go about your business while you are here," he added. "And we'll tend to our own."

I thought to myself that Dad uses his pipe to make a smoke screen whenever there is something unpleasant to be said, and he doesn't like to say it. He hides behind a puff of smoke and pretends we can't see him, like Robert playing hide and seek with me and Ednalice. He hides his face and thinks because he can't see us, we can't see him.

But it was wasted effort on Dad's part, I thought, to be concerned about offending Jack Meaders with his words. Jack smiled from ear to ear, just as though Dad had made him welcome with open arms.

"Speaking of tending to business," Jack said. "I'd better get to Oolitic before the post office closes, or I'll be out of business this week."

With another booming laugh, he shoved his chair back from the table. Linzy got up when he did and led the way to their living quarters.

Jack Meaders had to drive to the post office in Oolitic every Saturday to pick up his order of Watkins supplies and to get his paycheck, which came by mail to the general delivery.

One day, when I was staying with Grandma Stoner while he and Linzy went to town, Grandma told me that Linzy had to go along with Jack to make sure that he didn't drink up the money or gamble it away at cards. Linzy would cash the check at the bank, Grandma said, then allow Jack just enough money to live on while he was away from home.

"I made her do it that way." Grandma ground her gums as if chewing over her words. "Otherwise, there would've been no money left for her and the young-'uns," she had added.

Today was no exception. Shortly after they had gone to their rooms, Linzy and Jack Meaders came back to the kitchen, dressed and ready to go to town.

"If it's all the same to you," Linzy said to Mom, "we'll just leave Ednalice here. Jack wants to check at the courthouse and see if Grandma made any provisions for her farm. He figures that she might have left it to me." She looked down at her hands clasped tightly in front of her, then at Mom's face. "There's no telling how long that will take," she added. "And Ednalice would be plumb tuckered out before we get through with it."

Mom said that she and Dad had to go do their trading, but they would take Robert and Ednalice with them. "Set your mind at ease," she told Linzy. "The child won't be any bother at all."

chapter twenty-six

After telling Ednalice to behave herself and mind her manners, Linzy got in the car with Jack and they drove away. It wasn't twenty minutes later that Mom tucked the two kids into the back seat of the old Buick, and she and Dad left to do their trading in Oolitic. Even though Saturday afternoon was the one day that I looked forward to all week, this time, I offered to stay home and do the dishes and clean up the house while they were gone.

I finished washing and wiping the dishes and put them away. Then I swept the floors. I had just started sweeping the back porch when Johnny and Byron came whistling around the corner of the house.

"Hey, where is everyone?"

Johnny looked at the empty backyard, then toward

the kitchen door. "We saw Pa go by the sawmill more than an hour ago, and a few minutes later, Rob drove by. Ain't they home yet?"

"They've been here, but they've all gone to town."

I gave the steps a lick and a promise, then leaned the broom against the side of the house. "Did you want to see Jack?"

They both laughed as if I had made a bad joke.

"Not if we can help it," Johnny said.

Every morning since the fire, Johnny and Byron had come by our house on their way to work at the sawmill. Then when the five o'clock whistle blew at quitting time, they came back across the ridge and ate supper with us. Linzy Meaders said that the boys slept and changed their clothes at Aunt Fanny's house, but they lived at ours.

Johnny and Byron chopped the wood and kept the woodbox filled, carried in water, and cut the weeds while they were at our house. And they did anything else that Mom and Linzy asked them. But today, they made no move toward doing any of these things. The two of them dropped down on the porch steps, all out of breath, and Johnny said that this was without doubt the hottest day he had ever seen.

"I keep thinking how nice and cool it would be in the cave at the old blue hole," Byron said, not bothering to open his eyes.

"Yeah." Johnny rested his head against the porch post and closed his eyes against the sun. "But it would be a long hot walk to get there," he said.

I sat down between them and nudged Johnny with

my elbow. "I didn't know you boys had a cave around here. How come you've never told me about it?"

"It's not the kind of cave you'd think," Byron said. "It's nothing but a big hole in the rocks at the old stone quarry."

"All caves are big holes in something or other," I said. "And I'd like to see this one. The cave Jamie and I found was back in the hillside."

Johnny roused himself to say that I might as well forget it. We weren't going to the cave. "That quarry hole is no place for a girl," he said. "And besides that, it's full of water and we have to swim the blue hole to get to the cave."

"You're just like Mom!" I jumped up and stormed away from them. "She says I can't do anything that I'd like to do, just because I'm a girl."

I felt the sting of angry tears and brushed my hand across my eyes before the boys could see them.

Byron got to his feet and started toward me. Then he turned back to Johnny. "Now, see what you've done. You've made her mad at us."

"You started it." Johnny swore softly under his breath. "You shouldn't have brought up that damn cave in the first place."

They whispered back and forth so I couldn't hear them. Then they ambled over to where I stood scowling in the hot sun.

"We'll take you to the cave if it will make you happy," Byron said. "But on one condition: you'll have to promise not to tell your mom and Linzy that we went to the blue hole."

I promised and crossed my heart. "I'll not ever tell a living soul," I said.

Johnny said, "Hah," and struck off across the field ahead of Byron and me. It was a long walk, and a hot one, before Johnny finally pointed down the path and said, "There's the blue hole!"

The weeds and grasses that grew tall around the old quarry had been trampled flat on one side of the blue hole, and there was a hard-packed, bare spot of ground where nothing grew. It was here that Johnny and Byron took off their shoes and unbuttoned their shirts. When they reached for their belt buckles, I looked away.

"You're not going to take off your clothes, are you?"

"Sure," Johnny laughed. "You don't think we swim in them, do you?"

I started backing away from the edge of the quarry hole. "Then I'll not stay here," I said. "I'm going home."

Johnny caught me around the waist and yelled, "Last one in is a rotten egg!" And tossed me into the blue hole.

I gulped a mouthful of air just before I hit the water, but I sank like a rock and the air was all gone when I came to the top. I had gone swimming in Lick Crick with Jamie lots of times. But the creek had been shallow, and the only times the water came over our heads was when we purposely ducked each other. I had never been in water so deep that my feet wouldn't touch bottom, and I didn't know if I could really swim or not. But one thing I knew for sure and certain:

I was going to get out of this blue hole somehow. And when I did, I was going to kill Johnny Meaders for throwing me in here.

My waving arms touched something solid. Then I heard Byron say, "Hang on to me, Seely. I'll get you a foothold on the rocks."

I felt his hands lifting me, and the next moment I was standing on a huge block of stone that reared up from the water. Byron pulled himself up beside me, and when we had wiped our eyes so we could see again, he gave me a boost to the next piece of stone. From there I scrambled to the top of the rock pile. My scraped and skinned knees didn't slow me one whit. Getting even with Johnny Meaders kept me going. I told myself that I would make him sorry he ever laid a hand on me, if it was the last thing I ever did.

I jumped from the last stone into the high weeds on the bank of the blue hole, and there just a short sprint away stood the target of my anger, whooping and laughing at the trick he had pulled on me.

Without even thinking about what I was doing, I lowered my head and charged into Johnny like a mad bull, hitting him in the stomach with all my might. He bent double from the force of the blow, and his head came down hard as I lifted mine for another lick at him. Our heads came together with a solid crack that knocked me half senseless.

Johnny staggered backwards, grabbing me around the middle as he stumbled and dragging me down on top of him when he fell. I lay there a moment, trying to get my bearings, then I raised my head and pushed the wet stringy hair out of my eyes so I could see where to hit him again.

Johnny's face was directly beneath mine, and he lay as still as death. The whole lower half of his face was bleeding like a stuck hog on butchering day. His nose was mashed and his mouth split in two places where his teeth had gone through his lip.

I forgot that I was mad at Johnny, that I aimed to kill him if I could. I screamed for Byron, begging him to come and help.

Before I could call his name a second time, Byron was kneeling on the ground beside Johnny and me and mopping Johnny's bleeding face with his wet shirt.

"I didn't really mean to hurt him."

Byron didn't say anything. He just kept wiping at the blood as it seeped from Johnny's nose and mouth.

I tried to get up, but Johnny's arms tightened around me and I couldn't move. I braced my hands on the ground on either side of him to push myself away, and Johnny giggled.

"Promise me you won't hit me again, and I'll let you go."

"He's not hurt," Byron said, with a note of relief. "He's just playing possum."

He wadded the bloody shirt into a ball and tossed it lightly at Johnny's face.

When Johnny turned loose of me to catch the soggy, wet shirt, I rolled away and got to my feet. He sat up and grinned, then winced as his split lip opened and bled more freely.

209

"You sure do play rough," he said, his eyes laughing, teasing me, as he blotted his mouth.

"I should've done worse than that!" Now that I knew Johnny wasn't hurt bad, I was mad all over again. "Just look at me! What do you think Mom will say when she sees me looking like a drowned rat?"

They both turned and stared at my wet cotton dress, which clung to my body like a second skin. I folded my arms across my chest, then felt so awkward and foolish I let my arms hang loose at my side and clasped my hands together in front of me. I never should have asked them to look at me, I thought.

Johnny and Byron sat on the ground and laughed at my discomfort.

"It's not funny!" I told them. "Mom will have a fit if I go home like this."

The boys weren't smiling now. "We're all going to catch hell when we get home," Johnny said soberly. He threw Byron's shirt back to him and stood up. "I'm sorry I got you into this mess, Seely. I wasn't thinking about later when I threw you in the water."

I looked at the serious blue eyes, swollen nose, and puffy red lips, and I felt like crying. "I didn't think when I rushed you, either," I said. Then, because I didn't want him blaming himself and feeling bad, I said, "My dress is old and it will dry in no time at all. But we ought to do something about your blood-stained shirts."

"We could go to Aunt Fanny's and get clean clothes," Johnny said.

Byron shook his head. "We can't do that. If Aunt

Fanny ever found out that Seely came to the blue hole with us, she'd tell it all over the county. Then we'd be in worse trouble than we are now."

Byron was right. The fuss and furor would die down a lot sooner if the folks thought that no one else knew about our misadventure. But there was no reason why they should ever know, I thought. I knew one person who would sympathize with us. We'd be safe to tell her. And she would never breathe a word about it.

"Nellie Fender would help us," I said, breaking the heavy silence. "And she'd never tell a soul."

chapter twenty-seven

*J*ohnny and Byron looked at me as if they thought I had lost my mind. They started arguing against it before they had time to even consider what a wise move it would be.

I told them that, in the first place, no one would expect us to go to the Fenders. And secondly, it was closer to home. We could more than likely get cleaned up and be back to the house before the folks got home from Oolitic.

But they just stood and shook their heads no.

Finally, I said, "If you're both so scared of Schylar and Sylvester that you won't even go to Nellie's with me, then you can go home and take a licking from your dad. Anyone so stubborn deserves it," I added.

Without another word, I turned and started down

the path away from the quarry hole. I hadn't gone a dozen steps when Johnny yelled, "Hey, Seely, wait for me."

I stepped to one side of the path and waited until they caught up to me.

"Linzy says that you shouldn't roam the hills and hollers by yourself," Johnny said. "And besides that, you're going in the wrong direction." He pointed toward a ridge of hills off to the left of us. "Nellie Fender lives over that ridge."

This made the second time in as many days that I had lost my way in these hills, I thought, as I followed the boys across the field, into the trees, and over the far hill. "It's no wonder a person can't find their way around here," I muttered. "All the fields and trees look the same."

And they did. Every field and meadow was surrounded by tree-covered hills, one hill rising out of the ground on top of another, with no beginning and no end to the deep hollows that crisscrossed the hills, splitting them in two.

"No matter where I went when we lived at the old place, I didn't lose my bearings," I said to the backs of the two boys. "I could always find my way home through those woods."

Johnny and Byron turned and grinned at me, but they didn't say anything until we stopped about halfway down the other side of the hill. Then Byron pointed through the trees and said, "Seely, stop your belly-aching. You're not lost yet. There's the Fender house, right where we told you it would be."

The nearer we got to the Fender house, the more I wished that I had kept my mouth shut about going there. My dress was almost completely dry, and Johnny's red and swollen nose and mouth didn't look nearly as bad as they had at first. If Nellie happened to be away from home and the twins were there alone, we would be in more trouble than we could possibly handle.

I began to drag my feet. Johnny called me a slow poke and told me to get a move on or we wouldn't get there by dark.

"For someone who didn't want to go to Nellie's," I said, "you're almighty anxious to get there." Then just to rile him further, I added, "In case Schylar and Sylvester are at home, would you like me to go first and see if the coast is clear?"

Byron said, "You two stop your bickering. We go to the house together, or nobody goes."

"But what if the boys are there?"

"Then we won't stay."

I didn't argue with Byron any further.

Nellie Fender saw us coming and met us at the back gate. After one look at Johnny's face, her smiling welcome changed to one of concern. "Did you all run into my boys in the woods?" She seemed to hold her breath while she waited for one of us to answer.

Johnny grinned out of the good side of his mouth and jerked a thumb at me. "We ain't seen Schylar and Sylvester," he said. "Seely's the one who mashed my nose and mouth."

Nellie let her breath out slowly and moved closer

to Johnny. I saw him wince as Nellie touched his swollen nose, but she didn't seem to notice. She looked him straight in the eyes, and asked softly, "What did you do to her that she would turn on you?"

"He threw me in the blue hole!" I blurted, before Johnny had a chance to say anything.

Nellie smiled and smacked him lightly on the cheek. "I don't blame her. I'd have done the same thing." Then, "Come on in the house. I'll put something on that to take the swelling down."

Johnny held the cold compress that Nellie had made of Epsom salts and water to his face, while Nellie washed the blood stains from their shirts and hung them out to dry. I just spot-cleaned my dress. But after I had washed my face and combed my hair, Nellie said I looked almost as good as new. No one would ever guess that I had been dunked in the quarry hole.

I told Nellie that Mom would skin me alive if she knew I had gone there with the boys. She would never believe that I hadn't gone in the water on my own.

"Your ma is just taking care," Nellie said. Then she smiled and added, "But she'll not hear of it from me."

In no time at all, the wind had whipped the boys' shirts dry enough to put on. As Byron buttoned his shirt, he stopped pacing the floor and smiled for the first time since we had entered Nellie's house.

"Let's get out of here while the getting is good," he whispered, while Nellie was out of the room for a minute. "Old Schylar and Sylvester will soon be coming home for supper, and I don't want to be here when they do."

215

We hadn't seen any sign of them so far. But as Johnny said, there was no sense in pressing our luck further. We started out the kitchen door and almost collided with Nellie as she came hurrying inside.

Nellie seemed flustered about something and anxious to be rid of us. "You all had better get on home now," she said. "You're clean and dry, and Johnny's face looks as good as we can make it."

She sloughed off our thanks with a stammered, "It was nothing," and urged us on our way.

We headed for the back gate, but Nellie put her hand on Johnny's shoulder and stopped us. "Take the pike road and stay clear of the woods," she said. "It'll be safer for you all."

Nellie latched the gate behind us, then turned and went toward the house. We started walking quietly up the road. When we stopped at the top of the hill and looked back at the house, Nellie was nowhere in sight, but Schylar and Sylvester were leaving the woodshed that sat near the edge of the trees and heading straight for the kitchen door.

"I'll bet Nellie knew they were there," I said. "That's why she was in such a dither for us to leave."

We watched the Fender twins enter the house, then turned our steps toward home.

"Those two are a walking menace to the whole neighborhood," Byron said. "They ought to be locked up."

"Nellie told them that she would put them away for good, if they caused any more trouble around here."

Johnny said, as if he doubted my words, "When

216

did she ever say that?"

"She said so the day that Schylar and Sylvester . . ." I realized suddenly where my tongue was taking me and hushed.

"Well, go on."

"Came to our house," I finished.

Johnny and Byron gave me a look that said I didn't know what I was talking about and dropped the subject of the Fenders. I was glad they did. I never should have mentioned what Nellie had said to her boys. That was between the three of them. And none of our business.

When we passed the spot where the old truck had sat for so long, I thought of telling the boys what had happened to it. But that would've started them to talking about Schylar and Sylvester again, and I'd heard all I wanted to hear about them.

We had braced ourselves for a bawling out—or worse—from our folks, but we could have saved our worry for another time. We couldn't use any of the excuses that we had ready. There were no cars in the yard and no one at home, when we got there. With a great sigh of relief, Johnny and Byron dropped to their favorite spot on the steps and stretched their legs out in front of them.

"All that walking and stupid finagling so they wouldn't catch us in our wet clothes," Johnny moaned. "And now, they're not even home yet."

"Yeah, but they would've been," Byron replied, "if we hadn't done it."

I went on to the kitchen and started a fire in the

cook stove. Mom and Dad would be hungry and wanting supper as soon as they got home. And, I thought to myself, they wouldn't be nearly as apt to question what I'd been up to while they were away if there was a meal ready and waiting for them.

The boys helped me. When Dad pulled into the yard, with Jack Meaders close behind him, supper was ready to be put on the table for them.

Robert and Ednalice were wound up tighter than a toy top and too excited to eat. Dad and Mom had taken them to a baseball game at the county fairgrounds, and they were determined that we should know every detail of the game. No one had noticed Johnny's red nose and fat lip until Ednalice broke off her singsong chatter and asked abruptly. "Johnny, what has happened to your face?"

Jack Meaders had been telling Dad that sure enough, Old Lady Stoner had left the farm to Linzy, just as he'd figured. Mom and Linzy were talking quietly at the other end of the table. No one had been paying any attention to Ednalice's chatter. But at her question to Johnny everyone was suddenly quiet, their eyes riveted to Johnny's swollen face.

Johnny flushed red as the ripe tomato on his plate and put his hand to cover his nose and mouth. "I bumped it," he mumbled.

At the same time, I said, "I did it."

Everyone turned their eyes on me, and I explained. "We bumped heads."

Jack Meaders gestured angrily toward Johnny. "Did you bump it, or did the girl hit you?"

Johnny didn't say anything.

Mom said, "You answer him, Seely. And don't you story about it."

"Johnny bent his head down just as I raised mine, and he bumped his nose and mouth on my head. I wouldn't hurt him on purpose," I told them.

At Jack's disbelieving snort, Dad said, "Now wait a minute, Jack. That could be the truth." He pointed at me with his fork handle. "That girl's head is harder than tungsten steel." And then he added, "And just about as pliable."

Dad laughed quietly and went back to eating his supper, as if the matter was settled.

But Jack Meaders wouldn't let it be. He didn't ask Byron about it. He just kept digging at Johnny, implying that he was up to no good, or he wouldn't have been in a position to get hurt.

Finally, Linzy slapped the table with her hand and said sharply, "Jack, that's enough! There's one mad, one hurt, and one sorry this day. We'll hear no more about it."

Then more quietly, she added, "There's no call to run it into the ground."

Jack Meaders looked at his wife as if she had suddenly changed shape and color before his eyes. He opened his mouth a couple of times like a gaping fish out of water, but he didn't say anything more to Johnny.

I was surprised that no one had asked where we were or what we were doing when Johnny got hurt. But I guess they didn't think of it. That was the last we heard out of anyone about it. And soon afterwards, Johnny left the table.

He took his guitar from the pantry where he had left it the Saturday before, and he and Byron went to the back porch. In a little while, I heard the *plink, plink, plink* of the guitar strings as Johnny picked out a tune, and Byron's voice singing off key and humming the tune where he didn't know the words to the song.

The rest of us were still sitting at the dinner table when Gus Tyson and Aunt Fanny Phillips drove into the yard. Dad went to the door and asked them in, but Gus said they were on their way to Salem and had just stopped by to pick up Byron.

"His grandpa Winslow is feeling poorly," Gus Tyson told Dad. "And he wants to see the boy. We don't see the old man as often as we should," he added, "so I thought we'd drive down tonight and be with him all day tomorrow."

Gus touched Byron on the arm. "We'd best get started," he said, and turned back toward the car. Byron threw a fake punch at Johnny, slid off the step, and followed his dad. A moment later the car door slammed, the motor roared to life, and Byron was on his way to Salem with Gus and Aunt Fanny.

Johnny sat on the steps until the taillights of the car disappeared over the hill. Then he laid his guitar down and walked away into the darkness. I jumped from the far end of the porch and ran after him.

Johnny turned quickly as I stopped beside him.

"Seely?" Then, "What are you doing out here in the dark?"

"Nothing. I just wanted to walk with you."

"Then do it quietly," he said. "It hurts my face to talk."

His words reminded me of that moment on the bank of the blue hole when I'd charged into him and, suddenly, I didn't have a thing to say to Johnny. I wished that I hadn't ever followed him from the house. But now that I had, I didn't know how to walk away from him. If Byron was here, I'd just leave, I thought. But then, when Byron was with us, I never had any trouble finding something to say.

Johnny laughed softly and said, "You know, this is the first time we've ever been alone together."

I saw the flash of a match as Dad lit his pipe on the back porch. "We're not alone," I told Johnny. "Dad's right there on the porch."

"I didn't mean that," Johnny said. "I meant the two of us without Byron."

Just the mention of Byron's name made it seem as if he was right there with us. I took a deep breath, and I wasn't tongue-tied any longer. Johnny and I talked until the house got quiet, and the lamp wicks were turned low for bed.

Johnny slept on the daybed in the room at the foot of the stairs that night. He said it wouldn't bother him one whit that Grandma Stoner's corpse had been laid out in there.

"Her ghost might cross the room on its way upstairs

221

to haunt Pa," Johnny whispered. "But it wouldn't disturb my sleep." He nudged me and giggled. "I was always Grandma's favorite."

"You wake Dad or Jack Meaders with your foolishness, and you won't be anyone's favorite around here," I told him.

From her bedroom, Mom called, "Seely! Quiet down!"

I shoved Johnny into the room and closed the door behind him.

chapter twenty-eight

On Sunday morning, without Byron, Johnny wandered around the house like a lost soul. He sat at the table and ate ham and eggs with Dad and Mom and me, but he might as well have been munching hay for all the pleasure he showed in his breakfast. The minute Dad slid his plate away and reached for his pipe, Johnny left the table.

Later, after I had finished doing the dishes, I went outside. Johnny was sitting on the porch steps staring off into space as if he was the last one left in the world.

Stupidly, I said, "Hey, you look like you've lost your best friend."

He let his eyes rest in my direction, but his expression didn't alter. "Maybe I have," he said flatly.

I smiled and sat down as close as I could get to him. "You've still got me."

"You? A best friend? Hah!" His fingers touched his bruised lips, and his tone of voice told me that he didn't consider me a best anything. But I just ignored it.

"I'm the best you've got right now," I replied with spirit.

Johnny grinned at that, then laughed aloud as he smacked me lightly on the shoulder.

Before he could say anything more, Dad spoke from behind us. "Do you young'uns have anything hatched up for this morning?"

I moved away from Johnny, and we both stood up to face Dad.

"No, sir," Johnny said.

I just shook my head.

"I'll make you a proposition," Dad said, looking at Johnny. "You help me drag logs in from the woods and cut them to fit the cook stove, and I'll take you to the ball game this afternoon."

"It's a deal," Johnny said, and stuck out his hand to shake on it.

"I'll tell Mom that I'm going with you." I started toward the kitchen door.

"Seely, you're not going."

Dad's words stopped me in my tracks. I thought of the cool shade beneath the trees and the man-talk that I would miss and began to coax Dad to go with them. "I could be a lot of help to you," I told him.

"You'd just be in the way."

His voice was sharp with annoyance, but as I turned away, he said softly, "Seely, help your mother. Johnny and I can handle the logs."

Dad and Johnny left the house and headed across the field toward the stand of trees that lay to the east of us. Even though he stood as tall and straight as he could make himself, Johnny's dark head barely came to Dad's shoulder.

Somehow, I thought to myself, Johnny doesn't look nearly as tall and grown-up when he's with Dad, as he does walking beside Byron.

I shaded my eyes against the brightness of the early morning sun and watched as he stretched his steps to match Dad's long stride. Most of the time, Johnny was taking two steps to Dad's one.

I guess Dad must have noticed it. He slowed his pace so that Johnny wouldn't fall behind, and the two of them walked with the sun in their faces, leaving long shadows behind them to cover their tracks.

". . . like a blue-eyed Indian," Mom said, from close behind me.

I hadn't heard her come outside, and her words echoed through my head before I realized she was speaking to me. I let my breath out slowly and turned from the field.

Mom had a strange look on her face as her eyes rested first on me, then moved to follow Dad and Johnny into the woods.

"I didn't hear you," I said, lowering my eyes and defending myself against her look.

"I know you didn't," Mom replied. "You had your head so full of that black-haired boy that you wouldn't have heard the blast of Gabriel's horn."

She had me there. I couldn't deny that I had been thinking of Johnny Meaders and finding pleasure in the thought. I lifted my eyes to Mom's face just in time to catch the tail-end of her smile as she turned back to the kitchen.

I sat down on the steps, but it was too hot to stay there. I went to the kitchen. Linzy Meaders was fixing breakfast for Jack and Ednalice. I just said good-morning and passed on through the house to my room.

I thought Robert was still asleep, but as soon as I closed the door, he sat up in bed and said, "Seely, what time is it?"

I said, "Time you were out of bed." Then added, "If you hurry and get dressed, you can eat breakfast with Ednalice."

I thought that would get him up and out of the room, but he just rubbed his eyes and said, "What day is it today?"

"Sunday."

"How do you know it's Sunday?"

I could've said because Sunday always follows Saturday, but instead I chose to tell him, "There's a quiet about the day that lets us know it. All week long, when we wake in the morning, there's a busy feeling in the air. Like we've got to hurry and get things done. But when we wake on Sunday, we know that everything is caught up and there's nothing to do all day."

While I was speaking, Robert had got out of bed and put his clothes on. "There's something to do today," he said, smiling all over his face. "Dad said he'd take us to another baseball game on Sunday."

Robert tore out of the room like his britches were on fire, leaving me alone to think over what he had just told me.

It was plain to see that Dad had pulled a sandy on Johnny Meaders. He had intended to go to the ball game all the time. Yet he had led Johnny to believe that he was taking him as a special favor for helping to bring in the stove wood.

"That's downright sneaky!" I spoke aloud, talking to myself. But the room was empty. No one could call me on it.

We had an early dinner. Usually, we never ate before two or three o'clock on Sunday, but it wasn't yet noon when Mom and Linzy called us all to the table.

Robert bounced in his chair and whispered to Ednalice, urging her to eat faster so they could leave for the ball game. Finally, Mom lost her patience and threatened not to allow him to go to the game if he didn't behave himself.

"Now, you get up and sit down," she said, as Robert slid from his chair.

He stood for a moment as if undecided what to do. Then he said with exasperation, "Do you want me to get up or to sit down?"

Dad said, "Robert!"

Robert sat down. And he didn't move once nor open

his mouth, except to take a bite, during the rest of the meal.

Mom offered to help Linzy with the dinner dishes, but she shooed us out of the house.

"Jack will be busy sorting his Watkins orders," Linzy said. "I might as well be here in the kitchen out of his way."

Dad grinned and said we should get started before Linzy changed her mind, and everyone laughed. But I think he meant it. I figured he was just taking us to the ball game so he wouldn't have to be in the same house with Jack Meaders all day. Dad had never offered to take us to a baseball game before now. And the games had been going on all summer.

Mom and Dad sat in the front seat of the car, and we kids piled into the back. We hadn't gone three miles from home when Robert asked Johnny for the third time, "How much farther is it?" Johnny said, "Wait and see." Then he whispered to me that he wished he had ridden on the running board. "That kid could drive a wooden man nuts," he said.

I laughed and told Johnny that I'd known that for a long time. Then I moved closer to him to make more room for Robert and Ednalice.

The ball game was being played in an open field at the fairgrounds. And by the time we got there, the wooden benches, which were stacked around the ball diamond, were packed with people who had come early to see the game. Dad told us to wait for him near the stand that sold popcorn and candy bars, and he went to find us a seat.

Robert teased Mom for a chocolate bar until she fished a nickel out of her pocketbook and gave it to him to keep him quiet. Johnny moved away from us and stood looking in the other direction, as if he didn't want anyone to think he was with us. I was glad when Dad came back and said there was a place to sit on the very top row of seats.

"It will be hot up there," he told Mom. "But we'll be able to see every play."

I didn't get to see anything. I was kept on the move looking after Robert and Ednalice.

We had no more than got settled in our seats when Robert had to be taken to the pump for a drink of water and to wash his face and hands. Then after we had squeezed our way between the people and climbed to the top again, he had to go to the toilet.

I was coming back from the outhouse with Robert and Ednalice, and I suppose the game was half over, when the storm hit.

The wind came before the storm, whipping pieces of old newspaper and candy wrappers into the stands and stinging our eyes with dust from the ball diamond. Even our teeth had a gritty film from breathing the air.

Lightning flashed across the sky and the thunder crashed right on the heels of every fiery streak. Then the rain came in blinding sheets of water, taking our breath away and soaking us to the skin. Dad said, "Damn the luck," as he tried to push a path for us through the scurrying crowd. Some had made for the barn where the park implements were housed, but most of them, like us, headed for their automobiles.

Dad and Johnny fought the wind to get the ragged top fastened onto the car. Mom jerked the quilts off the seats, exposing the holes, and threw one to me. The quilts were only used to cover the seats when Mom was going to be riding in the car.

"Hold this over the windows," she shouted above the storm. But it was useless to try. The wind whipped the wet quilt into my face and the rain came in anyway. It came through the top, also. Mom tried to dodge the drops of rain, but every time she moved her head, water hit her in the face or ran down the back of her neck.

"If you were bound and determined to waste money on an automobile," she told Dad, "you could've got one with a solid top. This car is worse than none at all," she added.

Dad replied shortly that it beat the hell out of walking, and nothing more was said about the faults of the Buick.

When the storm had slacked off enough so that Dad could see the road, we started home. In some places along the way, Dad had to drive through water up to the running boards. And once we had to back up and go around to another road because a bridge was washed out. When we crossed White River, the rolling, muddy water was almost touching the wooden plank floor of the bridge.

The rain had stopped by the time we got to the lane that led back to our house, but the road was a loblolly of mud, and slick as a peeled grape. Dad pulled the car off the pike road as far as he dared, shut off the motor, and we stepped into ankle deep mud and water to get home.

Steam rose from the fields and trees and hung in thick layers like a gray wool blanket over the hills and hollows. From the top of the ridge, our house was almost completely hidden by the heavy fog.

Dad said he hoped that Gus Tyson wouldn't try to make it home today. "With this fog rolling in, he'd have no way of knowing about the bad washes in the road."

Johnny replied that one way or another, Gus would be at the mill when the whistle blew in the morning. "He expects the men to be on time, and he'll be there. And Byron with him," he added with a smile.

Jack Meaders was pacing the floor when we got to the house. He greeted Dad with, "How in the hell will I get that car out of here in the morning?" Then he looked past Dad's shoulder at the automobile as if he could wish wings onto his car and fly it out to the hard road.

"Dry as it's been," Dad said quietly, "the ground will soak up this water and the road will be passable. But that fog won't lift till after sun-up. And I don't aim to budge from here until it does," he added.

Jack Meaders allowed that Dad was right about the road and the fog. "Only a fool would venture out on foot in this," he said, "let alone behind the wheel of an automobile."

Johnny took a handful of rags and a scrub brush to

clean his shoes that he had left outside the door when he got home, and headed for the back porch. I stood in the middle of the room and looked after him. He closed the screen door quietly behind him, then I picked up my muddy shoes and started for the porch.

As we scraped mud from our shoes and tried to wipe them clean, I thought of the day last spring when Mom had said that I wouldn't have to wade mud to get to high school, and I laughed out loud. At Johnny's puzzled look, I explained. "Mom has promised me fair weather and dry roads when I start to high school, so maybe we won't have to clean muddy shoes then."

Johnny laughed. "It would be worth a lot if she can manage it."

"Was that little bit of ball game that you got to see worth all this?" I waved my hands to take in the muddy shoes and his wet, mud-smeared pant legs.

Johnny grinned and flipped a marble-sized mudball in my direction. "It wasn't just the ball game." He glanced toward the kitchen door and lowered his voice. "I guess I would have done anything to get out of staying here all day."

"But why?" I asked.

"Pa and me can't get along. He's ashamed of me because I won't fight the Fenders and keep running away from trouble. I'd rather just stay away from him than argue," Johnny said.

"You're just like Dad! I think that's the only reason he took us to a ball game today. Just so he wouldn't have to act sociable toward your pa."

I bit my tongue, but there was no way to take the words back. I felt my face grow warm and pink, as Johnny whooped with laughter.

"That's what I like about you, Seely," Johnny said, between gusts of laughter. "You say the truth even before you think it. You're a regular female honest Abe," he added.

"Don't you make fun of me, Johnny Meaders!"

I threw my shoes onto the porch and got up. "I don't have to sit out here and listen to you."

Johnny said, "Aw, come on."

But I stomped across the porch and slammed the kitchen door behind me.

"Seely, don't bang that screen door!" Mom didn't even turn to make sure it was me, but went on dishing up the supper. "And tell Johnny to come and eat."

I didn't bother to go to the door. I called over my shoulder. "Mom says come and eat, laughing boy!"

Under her breath, Mom said, "I don't know what's got into you lately."

That makes two of us, I thought. I don't know, either.

As much as I liked Johnny Meaders, it seemed like I couldn't get along with him for five minutes without getting mad at him about something. Yet, when he wasn't around, I couldn't stop thinking about him. Most of the time, like now, I wished he would fall off the porch steps and break a leg.

Robert and Ednalice fell asleep at the supper table and Mom put them both in Robert's bed. Then while

I was clearing the table, Johnny left for Jubilee. Jack Meaders told him that he had no business wandering around the country on a night like this, but Johnny said he wanted to see if Gus Tyson had made it back from Salem. "If Byron's home, I'll stay the night with him," Johnny said as he was leaving.

I was glad to see him go. All during supper, every time I looked up from my plate, Johnny had been looking at me. Once, he smiled and put his fingers to his sore lips and blew across them, as if sending me a kiss. I couldn't say anything then, but I frowned at him and didn't even glance his way again. I'll get even with him tomorrow, I thought.

Dad took his pipe and went to the porch to smoke. A few minutes later Jack Meaders joined him there. Mom said that I should go to bed. She and Linzy would do the dishes.

I was only too happy to go to my room and see the last of this day. As far as I was concerned, this Sunday had been a complete loss.

Robert and Ednalice didn't stir when I lit the lamp and closed the door to our room. I put on my nightgown, then blew out the light and got into bed. There was a faint sound of voices from the kitchen, but other than that, the house was quiet.

Outside the window, the crickets and katydids chirped and sawed away as if they were having the last concert of the summer and every insect from miles around had come to join in and help celebrate it. I closed my mind to everything but the sound of their music. It had nearly lulled me to sleep when I heard the Meaderses going upstairs to bed. My last thought of the evening was that Byron must have got home. Otherwise Johnny would've been back by now.

chapter twenty-nine

Mom and Linzy both overslept that next morning. It was broad daylight when I was awakened by the sound of Mom's hand slapping smartly on the Meaders' door to wake Linzy. I glanced across the room to where Robert and Ednalice were sleeping in Robert's bed. I thought sure the noise would waken them, but they didn't even stir.

Linzy's voice was fuzzy with sleep when she answered Mom, but it got clear and firm as she called Jack to get out of bed. I was up and had my clothes on when I heard her quick steps on the stairs as she hurried down to help Mom with the breakfast.

"I don't know when I've slept so sound," Linzy said, when we met at the door to the kitchen. "I feel rested this morning for the first time since Grandma Stoner was taken from us."

She didn't expect an answer, so I just smiled and followed her into the room.

Mom had a fire going in the cook stove already, and the coffeepot was making gurgling sounds on the front stove lid. Linzy made biscuits, Mom broke a dozen eggs in a bowl to scramble, and I set the table. By the time Dad and Jack Meaders got to the kitchen, we had breakfast ready and waiting for them.

I thought sure that Dad would yell about the time and raise a fuss because he was so late leaving for work. But all he said was, "It looks like we'll have a good day," and sat down to eat.

It did look like the beginning of a fine day. The heavy fog that had covered the hills when we went to bed had lifted, and all that remained of it was a slight haze between us and the sun.

Jack Meaders said the sun would soon burn the mist away. "And then, begging your pardon, Zel, it will be hotter than hell."

Dad and Jack were just leaving the house to go to work when Gus Tyson drove into the yard and slid to a stop no more than an arm's reach from them. Gus threw up his hand to hold them there, then got out of his automobile.

"Jack, you might as well unload your car," he said, his voice carrying well into the kitchen. "You'll not be making your rounds today."

Gus took Jack Meaders by the arm and, counting

Dad in by a nod of his head, he spoke low and earnestly to them. Mom and Linzy and I waited near the door, but we couldn't hear a word that was spoken.

Suddenly, Jack Meaders made a sound, as if the wind had been knocked out of him, and covered his face with his hands. Linzy said, "Something's happened to Johnny!" and ran out the door and down the porch steps before we fully realized what was going on.

Dad stopped Linzy's headlong rush toward them. He put his hands on her shoulders and spoke softly, as if gentling a wild colt to carry the weight of a saddle. At Dad's words, Linzy folded her arms across her stomach and bent over, as though she had been struck by a sudden cramp. She opened her mouth to speak, but no words came. Linzy shook her head as if to deny Dad's words, then straightened and slowly moved over to be near Jack.

Dad and Gus Tyson left the Meaderses together, alone in the yard, and came on toward the house. Dad's face was lined and empty, drained of everything but weariness, and his steps were those of a very old man whose years have suddenly caught up with him.

Once before, I had seen Dad when he walked as if he was tired to death, and the lines in his face were deep enough to bury my little finger. That had been when Jamie drowned in the flood of Lick Crick. I didn't want to know what had happened now to bring that look to his face again.

I started backing slowly away from the door, then turned and ran from the room. But I couldn't run far enough to get away from Mom's anxious voice as she questioned Dad, nor his answer.

"It's Johnny Meaders," Dad said, as if the name was choking him. "Gus found him dead, tied to the back bumper of our old Buick. Johnny had been dragged to death before the car was wrecked and left in a ditch near the White River bridge."

I covered my ears with my hands and pressed my face hard against the cool plastered wall. What Dad had said about Johnny couldn't be so. Gus Tyson had made a mistake. "I don't believe it," I said, moving away from the wall. "It's not so."

And that's what I told Gus Tyson when I faced him and Dad in the kitchen. "You've made a mistake," I said.

"Seely." Mom barely breathed my name. "Oh, Seely."

Gus Tyson looked at Mom, shook his head, then turned to me. "There's no mistake about it, girl," he said quietly. "The Fender boys confessed to me this morning how they stole your dad's automobile. Then when they came on to Johnny Meaders walking home from town, they said they jumped him, tied him fast to the bumper, and dragged him down the pike to White River."

His voice faded, and he had to clear his throat to go on. "We might never have known who did it," Gus said, "but Schylar and Sylvester got scared when they ditched the car, and they left tracks in the mud that a blind man could follow, straight from the wrecked au-

239

tomobile to Nellie Fender's back door."

Gus Tyson wiped his hand across his mouth as if to take away the bad taste of his words. "And that's where we found them," he added. "Hiding behind Nellie and begging her to make it right for them."

My eyes burned and my chest ached from holding my breath for so long. I wanted to scream, to yell and swear like Dad, against this pain I felt. But I knew better than to make a fuss. Mom would send me away. And I couldn't bear that. Now that I had heard this much, I had to know everything that had happened.

Mom said then, "Does Byron know?"

Gus Tyson nodded his head slowly. "We were coming in from Salem when we saw Rob's car and stopped to investigate. Byron was the one who found Johnny."

The sorrow in his face told us plainer than words ever could how Byron had felt at this discovery.

"Byron loosened the ropes that bound Johnny's wrists to the bumper and said he'd stay with him until help came. I notified the authorities, then Fanny and me followed the tracks to the Fenders." Gus Tyson hesitated a moment then. "Fanny felt that Nellie needed her there, so I came on alone to tell Jack Meaders about his boy."

He looked toward the yard where Jack and Linzy Meaders were standing close together, his arm around her and Linzy's head resting against his shoulder. I felt like we were spying on a private thing between the Meaderses, something not meant for our eyes, and I looked away.

Mom murmured that they would be needing coffee

and filled the percolator to the top with water. Then she dumped in a measured handful of coffee and dropped the glass-domed lid in place. She turned from the stove and seemed surprised to see me still standing there doing nothing at a time like this.

"Seely, get the young'uns up," Mom said gently, but firmly. "There'll be folks coming by soon to see the Meaderses."

I started to the bedroom, but she called me back. "Mind what you say." She cautioned me. "There's no need to tell them anything yet."

When I returned to the kitchen with Robert and Ednalice, the coffeepot had boiled over on the stove and the room was filled with the bitter smell of burnt coffee. Mom was outside. Aunt Fanny had brought Nellie Fender to the house while I was getting the kids ready for breakfast, and now everyone was gathered around Jack and Linzy Meaders in the back yard.

I put a bowl of oatmeal and a glass of milk in front of Robert and Ednalice and told them not to move from their chairs till I came back. Then I went to the door, closed the screen quietly behind me, and crossed the yard.

I stopped near Nellie Fender and put out my hand to touch her. But she was speaking to Linzy Meaders. I let my hand fall to my side and waited.

For just a breath in time, I thought it strange that Nellie Fender would have anything to say to Linzy right now. Then I realized that these two had the most to say to each other. They had both lost their sons. Nellie just as surely as Linzy. And even though I had considered Schylar and Sylvester of no account, I knew that Nellie loved them.

"They come a while ago and took my boys away," Nellie whispered. Then her voice got stronger as she stammered, "I should've listened to Gus and put them in a home when they were little, but I couldn't do it." Her eyes rested on Linzy's face, begging her to understand. "They were all I had in the world," Nellie said.

I thought the silence would last forever. Then Jack Meaders said, "Don't blame yourself, Nellie. It's not your fault."

Jack's voice always roared out like he was speaking from the next county, but not this time. I couldn't believe that he could speak so soft and gentle to anyone. I searched his face for some sign of the scorn and arrogance that I had come to expect from him, but all I found was sadness.

"I started this trouble when I laid the name bastard on your sons." Jack lowered his eyes as if he couldn't bear to face Nellie, and his voice dropped to a whisper. "I can't undo it," he said. "God knows, I wish I could. I want you to know I'm sorry for what I said, and I blame no one but myself for what has happened here."

I thought of Linzy saying, "One hurt and one sorry," and I knew it would take more than apology to heal this hurt.

Linzy reached blindly for Jack's hand and held it close.

Nellie was shaking her head. "No," she stammered. "This wasn't caused by what you said. It was jealousy. Pure, mean jealousy on my boys' part. They saw me making over Johnny the other day and thought I was taking his side, that I favored him above them. But they said they didn't aim to kill Johnny," she cried. "They only meant to scare him!"

Aunt Fanny put her arms around Nellie as she broke into tears. Mom moved nearer to Linzy. The men stood in awkward, uneasy silence and looked everywhere but at each other.

"The coffee is done," I blurted.

My voice sounded loud in my ears, and the words seemed to echo through my head. I felt like a fool. Then Mom said, "You all come in out of the hot sun and sit at the table."

She touched Linzy's arm and motioned for the others to come along.

Aunt Fanny said there was much to be done yet, and led Nellie, still crying, toward her car. Then Gus Tyson said he had to go to Oolitic. He had to get Byron and bring him home. Gus offered to drive Jack Meaders to the undertaker's to make arrangements for Johnny, and Dad went with them. Dad said he had to get that Buick hauled in to the junk yard. He never wanted to lay eyes on it again. Mom whispered something to Dad before he left. He looked surprised for a moment, but then he nodded his head and slipped a little black book in his shirt pocket. Only Mom and Linzy were left to drink the scorched coffee, and I don't think either one of them even noticed the bitter taste.

"I can't get by the thought," Linzy said, "that while Schylar and Sylvester were killing my Johnny, I was sleeping sound as a log. You'd think"—she sighed—"I'd have had some warning."

"It always seems to happen that way," Mom said. "I don't know why, but all our misfortunes seem to come between the dark and daylight. Tragedy comes creeping up on us while we're sleeping and unaware of the grief that awaits us in the morning." She moved her head sadly from side to side. "As if the pain will be more bearable," Mom said, "if we don't see it coming."

I didn't want to hear about the pain that sneaked in the night. I couldn't handle the hurt I had in broad daylight. I left Mom and Linzy sitting at the table and slipped quietly out of the room to find Robert and Ednalice. They didn't know about pain yet.

While I smoothed the beds, and made the house neat for company, I kept the kids close by me. I knew if they were with me, they couldn't mess things up behind me as fast as I cleaned. And besides that, their constant, carefree chatter held off the hurt that waited just at the edge of my mind.

chapter thirty

*W*e were sitting under a shade tree telling tall tales when the Reverend Mister Paully brought Dad and Jack Meaders home. Other than wondering why Dad and Jack weren't at work and what the preacher was doing here on Monday, Robert and Ednalice didn't question any of the goings-on.

"You stay here and think up another good story," I told them, "and I'll go find out why the preacher is here."

What I really wanted to know was why Gus and Byron Tyson hadn't come home with Dad. Surely Byron would want to be here, I thought.

I started to go in the front way, but as soon as my feet touched the porch, I heard the Reverend Mister

Paully's deep voice at prayer. I stepped to the ground and went around to the kitchen door.

I had hoped to get into the house where I could hear what was being said without anyone seeing me. But Dad was sitting on the back steps. He motioned to the empty space on the step beside him, and said, "You've no business in there now, Seely."

So I sat down beside him to wait till he thought I did have.

When the quiet between us had stretched to the breaking point, I said, "Why did the preacher bring you home? Why didn't Gus Tyson and Byron come with you?"

Dad gave me a long look, then said, more to himself than me, "I guess we'll have to talk about it." He ran his hand across his face, then turned toward the open field, his eyes on the woods beyond.

"The preacher was at the funeral home when we got there," Dad said. "He was waiting with Byron for the Meaderses to get there. Gus had to take Byron home. The shock of finding Johnny, then the long wait, had made the boy sick. Gus said on the way to the undertakers that he didn't feel right about leaving Byron to wait alone with Johnny. But be damned, if he knew how he could have kept him from it."

I waited awhile, hoping Dad would say without my having to ask. But when he didn't, I said, "When will they bring Johnny here?"

"They won't," Dad replied flatly. "Reverend Paully offered to hold a service for the boy in Jubilee, but Jack said they were moving back to Kentucky, taking

Johnny home to Kentucky for the funeral. All his kin are buried near Pineville," Dad added, "and that's where they figure Johnny's grave should be."

I thought of Jamie's grave, all alone and so far away in the Flat Hollow churchyard, and I knew the Meaderses were doing the right thing for Johnny. Even though they couldn't ever know it, I thought, boys shouldn't be buried among strangers.

My eyes started to burn and fill with tears. I slid off the step, mumbling to Dad that I had to get Robert, and ran toward the front of the house. I didn't know if the tears were for Johnny or just in remembrance of Jamie, but I couldn't let Dad see me crying.

The Reverend Mister Paully was leaving the house just as I rounded the corner, and I ran headlong into him. He caught and steadied me, then held me at arm's length while his piercing black eyes studied my face.

"Tears?" he asked gently. "Tears for Johnny Meaders?"

I shook my head and moved out of his reach. "I just don't like death and graves," I said foolishly.

I started to walk away, but the preacher fell in step with me. "Seely, maybe it would help if you thought of death as a deep, dreamless sleep and the grave as a covered bridge from light to light after a brief darkness," he said softly.

I had never heard the preacher speak in this manner. I wondered if he was reciting poetry or just repeating something he had read somewhere and saved in mind for such a time as this.

"It may seem like a long time for us," he went on,

"but for those who go there, it's only a brief moment. The light is never far away," he added.

"Do you really believe they will see the light of a new day?" I tasted salt on my lips and swallowed. "Do you?" I persisted.

"We've got to believe it," he said simply.

Jack and Linzy Meaders left our house early the next morning to drive back to Kentucky to bury Johnny. When Ednalice asked about him, Linzy told her they were sending Johnny home by train. "And we can't leave him waiting for us there at the depot," she said, as she hurried Ednalice toward the car.

The Reverend Mister Paully and Byron Tyson were the only ones to wait at our house to see the Meaderses leave. Gus Tyson had brought Byron with him earlier this morning as he came to wish the Meaderses good luck and God's speed to Kentucky. Then he had taken Dad to work when he left.

They had all been there the night before. Byron, with Gus and Aunt Fanny and the preacher, had come and brought a few members from the church. They had taken up a collection of money to give Jack and Linzy. "A little something to help with the cost of the funeral," the preacher had said.

Only Nellie Fender had been missing from the gathering. And Nellie should have been there, I thought. She needed someone, too.

Now, as the Meaderses were leaving the house, Mom put her arms around Linzy and held her close for just a moment. "If you ever want to come back," she said, "we'll be here. And you know as long as I have a home, you're welcome to stay." Mom slipped an envelope into Linzy's hand. "I've got no use for a treadle sewing machine," she said. "Use this money to buy a stone for Johnny."

I knew then it had been the bank book that Dad had slipped into his pocket before he went to Oolitic with Gus Tyson.

Linzy nodded her head as if she didn't trust herself to speak, hugged Mom again, then moved on toward the car. She stopped near Byron and looked long and steadily into his face. Almost as though she was memorizing every feature to take along with her to Pineville, Kentucky, and remember from now on.

But she didn't say anything to Byron, or even touch him.

I knew in my heart that when Linzy Meaders got in the car and drove away, she would never be back again. I think Mom must have felt the same way. As soon as the Meaders' car had cleared our yard, Mom took Robert by the hand and went into the house. She didn't even wait to wave Linzy out of sight.

But Byron and I, and the preacher, held our ground. I don't know why the Reverend Mister Paully felt that he had to see the Meaderses on their way. I suppose he had his reasons. And I had a good notion that Byron was here for the same reason that I was.

I knew for certain that I had to keep my eyes on Jack and Linzy for as far as I could see them. They were my tie to Johnny. When they were gone from sight, my last link with him would be broken. Then Johnny would really be gone.

For a while, I could see Ednalice waving good-bye from the back window. I answered her wave and smiled till my face ached. Then the car topped the rise in the road, and the sun made a splash of fire across the window glass, erasing her face.

"Well," the preacher said, when the Meaders' car had vanished over the hill in the blaze of sun, "I've another visit to make yet this morning."

He spoke as if he was begging our pardon for leaving so soon after the Meaderses.

Byron nodded a couple of times. "I know," he said. "I know."

The Reverend Mister Paully went on his way then, heading slowly across the open field toward the sweet gum trees and the short cut that led to Nellie Fender's place.

"Nellie is going to need more than an occasional call from the Reverend Mister Paully to fill her days," Byron said, his eyes on the departing figure of the preacher. "Jack and Linzy Meaders have Ednalice to care for, and though I'll never have another friend like Johnny, you're here with me. But Nellie Fender doesn't have anyone, now."

Byron's brown eyes were soft and sober as he turned to face me. "You understand, don't you, Seely? With Schylar and Sylvester gone, Nellie will have no reason to get up in the morning, not unless someone gives her a purpose." He looked toward the preacher, then back to me. "Nellie used to take care of me," he said. "Now she needs some care."

Nellie had taken care of me this summer, I thought to myself. I told Byron of the days when Nellie had walked with me through the woods, then waited to see me safe home. "Maybe, the two of us together can give meaning to her days," I said. "Her house is the only one between yours and mine, and on our way back and forth, we can always stop at Nellie's and keep her from getting lonely."

Mom called, "Seely, you and Byron come to breakfast."

"You go on," Byron said, as Mom called my name again. "I'm going to catch up with the preacher."

The Reverend Mister Paully had reached the trees and started down the path. His black coat was just a shadow in the woods. Byron lifted his hand in farewell and took off running toward the dark figure of the preacher, and I turned toward the kitchen door.

It was going to be another hot day, I thought. But for me, the summer was over and done with.